Night Rituals

Also by Michael Jahn

The Quark Maneuver (Edgar Award Winner)
Armada
Killer on the Heights
Kingsley's Empire

Night Rituals

A NOVEL

■

Michael Jahn

W·W·Norton & Company

New York   London

The text of this book is composed in 11/14 Janson Alternate, with display set
in Aquarius.
Manufacturing by The Haddon Craftsmen, Inc.

First Edition
Library of Congress Cataloging in Publication Data
Jahn, Michael.
Night rituals.
I. Title.
PS3560.A35N5 1982   813'.54   82–8277

ISBN 0-393-01630-7

W.W. Norton & Company, Inc., 500 Fifth Avenue, New York, N.Y. 10110
W.W. Norton & Company Ltd., 37 Great Russell Street, London WC1B
3NU

1 2 3 4 5 6 7 8 9 0

For Joe and Anne

Night Rituals

Anita DeMarco spent the last two hours of her young life learning how to make Hawthorn jelly at a natural cooking class at St. Dominic's Parish House. Her parents both worked late, and felt a thrice-weekly cooking class was just what their twelve-year-old daughter needed to stave off boredom. Anita liked it, too, so much so that as she walked home along Riverside Park's upper mall singing to herself, she was unaware of the man who had crept up from the depths of the park to kill her.

The mall was deserted, except for a far-off jogger making the turn around the Soldiers and Sailors Monument. It was a cold night late in March, and Anita held the jar of still-warm jelly under her coat. To her left, an occasional car moved slowly past the stately turn-of-the-century buildings on Riverside Drive. To her right, the park swept down to the Hudson River. An old stone-block wall separated the upper mall from the dark woods and glades below.

The wall was high enough and thick enough to protect a Plantagenet castle. Gloomy, algae-lined stairways led down to the roller-coaster hills, fields, and dark places that made up the main body of Riverside Park. The upper mall close by the aging gentility of Riverside Drive, was cobble-stoned, and laced with wooden benches. Anita DeMarco passed a woman who was walking a wire-haired terrier, and an old man smoking a meerschaum filled with scented to-bacco. But she made a turn and the wind came up, and she was alone again.

She wouldn't have seen her killer anyway. Dressed in black, he slouched against a lamppost marking one of the infrequent stairways. With the lamp knocked out, he was indistinguishable from the other shapes and shadows that kept people out of the park after sundown.

The jogger was around the Soldiers and Sailors Monu-ment and no longer in sight. Another was coming up from the south, but he was a half-dozen blocks away. The woman with the wire-haired terrier had crossed Riverside Drive and disappeared into an apartment building.

Anita thought of Spanish shredded beef and rice. She thought of the corn bread her mother had promised to make, and how good the Hawthorn jelly would taste on it.

The figure by the lamppost moved fast for his size. A hand smothered Anita's mouth and the scream that would have come from it. As she was dragged off, down into the dark-ness of nighttime Riverside Park, the jar fell to the cobble-stones and shattered.

HITLER'S REVENGE

Donovan saw the pigeons as tiny Messerschmitts blitzing his windowsill. True, he was overly fond of war movies, and apt to have such visions. But the birds *were* being unreasonable. Out of the hundreds of thousands of windows on Riverside

Drive, they chose to pick on his. And his bedroom window at that.

They were efficient and relentless. They swooped in at forty miles an hour, good speed for a bird, dropped their loads, then frequently landed to inspect the damage. Donovan hated them and was always concocting schemes to get rid of them. This particular day, though, he had to settle for bouncing an empty beer can off the window, a tactic which had no effect whatsoever on the pigeon sitting there. The phone was ringing off the hook. Despite his efforts to prove it wrong, the world needed him.

WHAT ARE COPS FOR?

Lois Regan called to say that Jack had done it again.

She had supported him all the years of their marriage, while he was working on his doctorate at Columbia. She even spent a year with him in a Quonset hut on the Bahía de la Campeche, Mexico, while he studied Mayan art. Since returning to New York, Jack had taken ten years so far to write his dissertation. All that time, he'd done things like stay out all night, not coming home until eight in the morning, then telling Lois he'd been to the library.

The dissertation still unwritten, Jack had some months before taken a job as a camp counselor in the Catskills. Lois called Donovan to say she'd found out Jack had been spending time with a girl from Iona College.

Lois threatened to divorce him, and Jack told her if she did she'd have to pay him alimony. She had, after all, accustomed him to being supported. Jack cited the recent Supreme Court decision backing alimony for men.

"I want you to take out your gun," she said. "Then I want you to shoot him."

"I can't," Donovan responded. "The department frowns on shooting friends' husbands."

"Come on," she insisted. "I need your help, and what are cops for anyway?"

"I have to go. There's been a murder in the park, and I'm expected to attend."

PARA LOS MUERTOS

The nude body had light olive skin and raven black hair. She lay at the foot of a tall, old maple in a grove of trees not far from a stairway. Around her in a circle measuring perhaps twenty feet across, the beer cans, candy wrappers, condoms, and other typical trash of the park floor had been decorously swept up.

Anita's head rested on a soft bed of white violets. Her face was expressionless.

"*Flores,*" Donovan said.

"*Para los muertos,*" Jefferson agreed, looking up briefly from his clipboard.

"Who is she?"

"Anita DeMarco. We found her clothes rolled up in a neat bundle." He pointed to a spot a dozen yards away, where the young girl's clothing was bundled as if for the laundromat. "She's thirteen . . . goes to the local public school. Lives on Eighty-fourth Street off Broadway. Her father is a packer at the A&P on Amsterdam. They reported her missing last night at midnight."

"What the hell was a girl her age doing out at night in this neighborhood?" Donovan asked.

"On her way home from a class at St. Dominic's Church. You know, they got all this fancy do-this and do-that shit up there? Learn how to bake a cake, clean out your own pipes . . . everything. Well, she went trottin' on home at about ten o'clock carryin' a bottle of jam she made at this cookin' class. The jam's up the steps there, did you see it?"

Donovan said that he saw it.

"She never made it home."

"Gotcha," Donovan replied.

"The Mex says it looks like she wasn't raped," Jefferson said.

The Mex is the medical examiner, not a Mexican. Donovan only knew of one Mexican in the neighborhood. He was a medical man, too.

"She was killed by a single knife thrust to the heart. But there is a slice on one wrist, and it looks like she was spread-eagled and held down, hands and feet, when she got it. There are bruises on the wrists and ankles."

Thomas Lincoln Jefferson was Donovan's assistant, a sergeant. They were close friends, a black sergeant and his Irish lieutenant, though it didn't often seem that way. Jefferson got his odd name when his father wanted to honor both namesake presidents, but without using the name "Abraham." He was afraid it would make his son sound Jewish. Donovan solved the problem of nomenclature by calling Jefferson "Pancho." Jefferson was known to despise Hispanics.

Donovan knelt and examined the body, looking at the bruises and touching the soft, cold, olive skin. Then he stood.

"Cover her up, will you?" he said in disgust. "You want me to throw up on the body?"

Gallows humor is often the first refuge of the cop who is

too easily upset. Gallows humor and artificial hardness. When presented with a ghastly scene, he either makes jokes or goes crazy.

Jefferson motioned to a uniformed cop, who pulled a plastic sheet over what remained of Anita DeMarco.

"Rican?" Donovan asked.

"Could be. I can't tell one from another. No, come to think of it, she's Cuban. One of the patrol cops said that, anyway. What the fuck difference does it make?"

Donovan shrugged, and looked around the crime scene. Uniformed cops and white-coated technicians crawled over the terrain like ants. Brown-suited detectives peered under rocks and turned over leaves. A photographer was packing lenses, cameras, and lights into a large, battered leather case.

"Decent of the murderer to clean up the garbage before laying the girl out. Look at this area he swept up! It looks like a halo around her. Is it swept up under the body, too?"

"Yeah. He must have prepared the site before grabbing her."

"At least the prick is neat. I like the way he bundled up the clothes, too. Any sign of the murder weapon?"

Jefferson shook his head.

"He must have taken it home to be polished," Donovan said. "Jog my memory, Pancho . . . this doesn't remind me of anything I've seen before in these parts."

"It beats me, too."

"It's a ritual killing, I suppose. Christ, I think I'd feel more comfortable with a good old rape-murder."

"Amen to that, brother."

"Have we found anything other than the clothes and the body?"

"The jam jar."

"That it, huh? Well, tell the boys to keep looking. They

can suspend the leaf-by-leaf, but I'd like to know if anything major comes up. You take care of the parents, then you can split."

"Sho' thing, boss," Jefferson replied. Like Donovan, he was itching to get out of there and was relieved to find it soon would be possible. When happy about anything, he was apt to put on an Uncle Tom act to remind his friend that he wasn't anything resembling Hispanic. Even the agony of seeing the parents of the dead girl was tolerable once he knew he'd soon be getting away from the scene of the crime.

"I'll see you at the office in an hour," Donovan said.

"Where you going?"

"To get a drink. I got one fuck of a hangover, and this ain't helpin' it."

"INFLATION HITS THE BAR BUSINESS TOO,"
HE SAID

Drunkenness is the second refuge of the cop who is too easily upset. The twentieth century teaches us not to care about our fellow man. Some of the old-timers like Donovan don't learn so good.

"A dollar forty-five for seven-eighths of an ounce of Jack Daniels is too much," Donovan said.

"That's what the price is," George the bartender replied stoically.

Donovan brandished a pocket calculator. "That works out to fifty-three dollars and two cents for a quart."

George was unimpressed. "Are you drinking or jerking off?" he asked.

"A bottle of Schmidt's. I think I can afford that."

The bottle was produced and poured.

"Ninety cents. The price is up a dime."

Donovan put a five-dollar bill on the bar and watched as a chunk was taken out of it. It was ten in the morning, and half the fifteen customers in Riley's were watching "Family Feud." Those customers who weren't trying to outguess the contestants on the game show were hunched numbly over their drinks. Above the bar, a long row of neon-colored signs announced the new prices. Donovan waggled an admonishing finger at the signs.

"With prices like those you don't brag. I can get a better drink for less at Sardi's."

"So go to Sardi's," George said, pouring a glass of beer for himself and sipping it.

"I thought bartenders aren't supposed to drink on the job."

"You also think you're gonna get a better drink for less money at Sardi's. What's the matter with you today?"

"A little Cuban kid got her ticket punched in the park."

"You talking about this park?"

"No, I'm talking about some park in Hoboken. It happened right in front of my building. I could almost see it from the window." Donovan told the bartender the basic facts of the case.

"There would have been more than one killer, right?" George postulated, upon hearing the evidence that the girl had been held down while stabbed.

"Looks that way," Donovan replied.

George trudged off to pour some vodka into an electrician who already had more of it than he needed. By the time four or five more customers had been serviced, Donovan was finished with his beer.

Above the bar, pasted to the mirror near the cash register, was a sign advertising two glasses of sangría for a dollar.

"Give me two sangría."

"It's your funeral."

George the bartender took out a slim, three-ounce wine glass and filled it with maroon liquid poured from a gallon jug that had no label.

"This is it?" Donovan said disdainfully, looking at his purchase. "Six ounces of cheap-shit Spanish wine for a dollar?"

"It's the biggest bargain on the West Side. After you've drunk this and thrown up, I come back and refill your glass for free."

George was a big man, six-foot-three at least, and in his late forties. He grew hair the way a garden grows weeds. It sprang from every inch of him. His facial features struggled to be seen beneath a brown beard that gave him the look of a mountain man. A brass belt buckle proudly proclaimed itself a souvenir of the Pro Football Hall of Fame in Canton, Ohio. George was a forceful presence; only a bit of North Korean hand grenade still embedded in his knee prevented him from swaggering.

"I had one fuck of a day yesterday," he said.

George's last name was Kohler. He was German.

"What happened?"

"You know Big Harold? The war hero?"

Donovan said that he knew. Everyone on Broadway knew Harold Gillis, the self-proclaimed hero of the American submarine service. He was occasionally called Big Harold to distinguish him from Little Harold, the diminutive, vodka-drinking electrician who worked over at the American Museum of Natural History. Gillis claimed to have been the torpedoman aboard the American submarine that sank the Japanese battleship *Yamato*, the most powerful battleship ever built. Any Riley's customer foolish enough to point out that the *Yamato* was sunk by American aircraft, not a submarine, was subject to the outraged vengeance of Big Harold's massive fists. Big Harold was generally ignored, when it was possible.

"Yesterday he got into an argument with this Rican. I

don't even remember what they were arguing about. The Rican pulled a knife and threatened to cut Harold open, right over there by the pinball. Now, you know that Harold can get really wild. Remember that time the guy came in with the monkey? Well, this time Harold didn't do anything. When the Rican waved the knife, he didn't even flinch. He just backed out the door and walked away."

"You were lucky."

"You bet your ass I was. I couldn't believe how lucky I had gotten. Big Harold is a *strong* motherfucker, on top of being big. So the Rican puts the knife away and goes back to his sangría—the same shit you're drinking. I'm just about to think the argument is over when I look out the window and see Harold crossing Broadway. He'd gone back to the building on Riverside where he works, gotten a chain saw, and has it slung over his shoulder. He's gonna turn the PR into taco sauce."

"What happened next?" Donovan asked, with mild interest. This sort of thing went on at Riley's with some regularity.

"I called the cops, what the hell do you think? Your brethren from the Twenty-fourth Precinct got here just in time. It took eight of them to haul him off."

"You lead some life," Donovan said.

"Yours don't seem like such a bargain," George replied.

NO LEADS

There was absolutely nothing to go on. That was how Donovan thought about the task of finding Anita DeMarco's killer. The death of one little girl might be tragic for her family, but New Yorkers tend to view such occurrences as the price to pay for living at the center of the known universe. This attitude is common on the West Side, the place in New York where teeming humanity teems the hardest.

The West Side stands between two parks: Central and Riverside. Its northern boundary is the assemblage of educational institutions surrounding Columbia University; its southern the cultural landmark of Lincoln Center for the Performing Arts. Broadway is the West Side's aorta. The four-lane highway with the decaying garden malls at the middle connects a dozen neighborhoods housing people from all parts of the earth. This isn't the Broadway of bright lights and glitter. It is the Broadway of Irish bars, Jewish delis, Spanish bodegas, and Chinese restaurants; of Cuban travel agents, Thai butchers, and stationery stores in which gambling parlors flourish openly. Donovan was not much interested in gambling. His specialty was murder, which he knew was the ultimate insult to his belief that good people should live forever.

NOBEL LAUREATES AND NUMBERS RUNNERS

There wasn't any more crime on the West Side than in any other Manhattan neighborhood. There was, for the most part, a good deal less. But crime on the West Side was noticeable. New York was the center of the world's media, and many of that industry's chronically underpaid toilers made their homes within a stone's throw of Broadway. Hiding the news of a murder from the press was like trying to hide Kareem Abdul Jabbar at a midget's convention. A few years back, the mugging murder of a prominent Israeli diplomat outside a Broadway Chinese restaurant caused enough of a flap to move the city government to action.

The mayor got together with the police commissioner and, while TV cameras rolled and reporters poked microphones in their faces, announced the formation of the West Side Major Crimes Unit, Lieutenant William Donovan, commander. For eighteen years, Donovan had been the most visible cop on the West Side. For twenty-two years before that, his father had the same role. Donovan was thirty-eight and handsome, with a commanding look and the ability to speak to both Nobel laureates and numbers runners. He was so much respected on the street that his eccentricities were, in the main, forgiven.

The headquarters of the West Side Major Crimes Unit was a large, single room on the second floor of a building on the west side of Broadway south of Eighty-seventh Street. Beneath it was a pawn shop, Riley's, a Szechuan restaurant, and a numbers parlor. The unit shared the second floor of the building with the local office of the Beneficial Finance Company. That last fact, Donovan liked to point out, "says more about the true nature of detective work than anything Conan Doyle ever wrote."

BASEBALL, BASKETBALL, FOOTBALL, AND HOCKEY

It was all according to the season. Jefferson was something of an electronics genius, and managed to wire up the computer display so that it got ball games. The dozen men who worked in the room appreciated the convenience. The patch to the central NYPD computer was taking the day off most of the time anyway, and diversion was often needed.

At the moment, though, the computer was going continuously, making comparisons between the DeMarco case and possible similar crimes nationwide. The West Side was truly an immigrant neighborhood, and there was always the chance the murderer brought his madness from a home far away. Two of Donovan's men watched the monitor and made relevant notes. Three others were up at Anita's school, talking to her friends and classmates. Two more were at St. Dominic's, talking to those who were on hand during Anita's last class. Another planted himself by the Soldiers and Sailors Monument in Riverside Park, stopping joggers and dog walkers to find out if any of them had seen a suspicious person that night.

Nobody saw anything. Nobody knew anything. Even the computer offered no helpful suggestions. Six days after Anita DeMarco breathed her last, Donovan was no closer to a solution than he might have been if he had just stayed home and watched TV the whole time.

FORTY BUCKS FOR FIFTY MINUTES

"I get forty bucks for fifty minutes," Donovan said, handing his friend a can of beer and sitting beside him on the couch.

"What?" Jack asked.

"That's for psychotherapy, of course. Full analysis will cost you extra."

"Okay," Jack laughed, "so you figured out I want to talk about my problems with Lois. Are you going to listen to me or not?"

"You keep it interesting and I'll listen."

"I know she came to see you. She found out I've been seeing a girl from upstate."

"So? With the preposterous stories you've been feeding

Lois to explain your staying out all night, you have to expect
to be caught now and then."

"I know, but it's always a shock when it happens. Look,
I *love* Lois, I really do. But we've been together ten years,
and it's gotten, well, *boring*. I'm not getting any younger,
Bill. Do you know I'll be thirty-three in a week?"

Donovan thought, but only for an instant, that he would
do as Lois asked and shoot Jack. Donovan was nearly thirty-
nine. He settled for snarling, "Yeah, sure."

"Lois is a wonderful girl, but . . . do you mind my saying
this? She's very old-fashioned and I'm sick to death of
straight fucking. You know, the missionary position and all
that? I want some excitement before I die. Suzanne—that's
my friend from upstate—is different, really wild. I mean, is
there anything wrong in enjoying myself?"

"No, as long as you don't mind *supporting* yourself."

Jack thought a moment, then said, "There's no chance
Lois will leave me. I've been driving her to do it for years,
and she never has. I think I'm safe."

"Famous last words, my friend. Why don't *you* leave *her*
if life is so boring? Move in with Suzanne."

"I'd have to leave New York," Jack replied, aghast. "I'd
have to move out of this building. God, I've been here ten
years. I can't imagine living anywhere else."

Donovan smiled, and said, "If staying in your old apartment is more important than new sexual positions, you're
incorrigibly married. Why don't you try buying Lois
flowers and champagne and seeing if she can't learn some
new tricks?"

"It's out of the question. She just isn't built for speed. And
I don't know that I'm incorrigibly married. I can support
myself if I put my mind to it. I've been working at Columbia
this semester, just a few hours a week, but there might be

more. And I can always wait on tables if it comes to that."

Donovan sipped his beer, and then asked, "What do you want me to say? Am I supposed to approve of what you're doing?"

Jack shook his head. "Don't say anything. Just listen. I want to tell you about Suzanne." And he went on to do it.

On the last night of her life, Nina Delgado spent three hours at a friend's apartment, studying for a test. Neither she nor her friend were any good at math, and even at Public School 487 they were expected to know at least a little. This was Friday and the test was not until Monday, but Nina was determined to get her average up and, in two years, have a shot at a higher education better than the one provided by automatic admission to City College.

The friend lived on Seventy-seventh off Riverside and Nina, on Ninety-third. It was a warm night and, not having change for the bus, Nina decided to walk up the mall. The death of Anita DeMarco was a week old and generally forgotten by the public. The mall was thick with joggers, dog walkers, and strolling couples. At eleven in the evening, Nina was sure there was nothing to worry about.

The man who had come up from the depths of the park to kill her waited at a different spot this time. This entrance wasn't steep like the others, but gradual. The steps were broad, curving, and took several hundred feet to descend the forty feet from the mall to the park. On their way, they curved around a large, square parapet built into the wall as an overlook. From it, one could look down on the abyssal darkness and, beyond, to the sparkle of lights reflected in the Hudson.

There was a stout tree at arm's length from the parapet. The killer climbed the wall, moving with slow, deliberate stealth. Soundless and practically invisible, he wedged himself between tree and wall and waited, just beneath the top, for the right person to come along.

The Delgado family apartment was nearby. A handful of blocks up from the Soldiers and Sailors Monument and halfway down Ninety-third Street, and Nina would be home. But she stopped, as she often did, at the overlook.

The view of the river was splendid, especially in March, when the absence of leaves on the many trees made it easier to see the shapes of the freighters plying the Hudson. She looked down for a moment, then turned, sat atop the wall and lit a cigarette, her only vice. A jogger went by and made the turn towards the monument. Two more went off in the other direction, southbound. A Number 5 bus picked up a solitary passenger waiting at the stop across the mall. Traffic was heavy on Riverside Drive, and the bus chugged slowly off.

Nina blew out a wisp of smoke, closed her eyes and savored the cool sting of the March air. Just then the huge and muscular arm enfolded her, lifted her like a twig, and pulled her backwards over the edge of the stone wall.

BURNT OFFERINGS

It was three in the morning, and Donovan was watching an episode of "Rat Patrol" while killing a six-pack and eating cold pizza. He liked that show for several reasons. First, it was relaxing to watch Sergeant Troy, his three men, and two jeeps beat the crap out of Rommel's Afrika Korps. Second, in some of his many weak moments, Donovan fancied himself as looking like Christopher George, the show's star.

He was profoundly pissed off when Sergeant Jefferson beat on the door to tell him there had been another murder.

She was a beautiful girl, a bit older than the first one, with darker olive skin. A black couple, teenagers both, who came over from Amsterdam Avenue to drink and fuck in the secluded woods had found her in the early morning hours.

She was laid out like Anita DeMarco, in a circle swept clean of debris. Her clothes were bundled and tucked inside a thicket of wild blackberries. Black hair which should have hung to her waist was fanned out beneath her lifeless head. Under that was a circular patch, made with consummate skill, of kernels of corn which had been stood on end and pressed into the soft forest loam.

The arc lamps set by police technicians illuminated the park for blocks, including the single puncture wound in the smooth mound of her virginal breast.

Donovan looked into Nina Delgado's lifeless eyes, then walked ten yards down the hill, unzipped himself, and pissed on a stripling maple.

"I can't stand it, Pancho," he said when it became obvious that Jefferson had followed him. "Tell me it ain't happening."

"She has the same marks as the last one. A slice on her left wrist, and bruises on wrists and ankles. You wanna put it back in your pants, lieutenant? I got to maintain my dignity. It's tough enough working for a white guy."

Donovan rezipped. "Any bleeding anyplace?"

"Some from both wounds. Not a lot, though."

"Name?"

"Nina Delgado. She's fourteen and lived on Ninety-third. I don't know what her father does for a living, and the parents haven't been told. You wanna take this one?"

Donovan shook his head. "One of the privileges of power is that you don't have to wipe off the victims' tears. Take the lieutenant's exam some day. You'll see."

Jefferson grunted, and tapped his pencil impatiently on his clipboard.

Donovan led the way back to the body, which Jefferson had the good sense to have covered. "What do you make of the corn kernels?"

"Beats me."

"They must have taken a lot of time to set up," Donovan said. "At least half an hour. Add another half an hour to sweep up the garbage in this place. And how much time snatching the girl? There's another thing—the corn isn't pressed down much directly under her skull. So you have to figure he killed her a little to one side, then when she stopped moving, lifted her here. All this crap is time consuming."

"Where the hell did he get it?" Jefferson asked.

"Precisely. I figure this all takes an hour to set up and at least half an hour to execute. You mean to tell me nobody comes along in that time?"

"Into the park? At night? You got to be crazy to come into this park at night."

"Somebody does," Donovan said ruefully.

"I can see takin' a stroll on the mall . . . but goin' down below, into the park proper? Fuck you, Jack."

"The distance between here and the mall, where all the joggers are, is maybe forty feet."

"The distance between humanity and barbarism," Jefferson went on, waxing eloquent as he did every now and then.

"I mean, a lot of crazy shit went down on the wrong side of the Great Wall of China. That's why the Chinese built the fuckin' wall. You think this here wall's a goddam decoration?"

Donovan had thought that, but felt it was wise to keep it to himself.

"Do we have any Haitians on the force?" he asked.

"Could be. We have some of just about everything."

"Dig one up for me."

"Why?"

"I drink at Riley's with this guy who cleans up the park. You know, sweeps shit off the ground. He says Haitians have these voodoo ceremonies with doves and candles..."

"Doves?"

"Okay, pigeons and candles. Why quibble? The point is that he's seen kernels of corn in their rituals. See if we have any Haitians on the force. They may know about it."

"Sure thing," Jefferson replied, scribbling on his clipboard. "You know, if this is a ritual involving a number of people, it cuts down the time setting it up and carrying it out."

"And so it does," Donovan nodded.

Sergeant Jefferson finished making his note. "There's one more thing. We found something strange. A burned spot. It's twenty feet to the south, between two roots that grow above ground."

"So what? Maybe someone had a barbecue."

"This was burned just recently, in the past few hours. It looks like strips of something were set on fire. Should I have the stuff taken to the lab?"

"Yeah, and check the DeMarco site again. Let's see if it was done there, too."

Jefferson led the way to the burned spot. It was circular, like the halo of corn kernels, and about a foot across. There was a slight mound in the center, where the outline of a material of some kind was visible.

"After it cooled, it was covered with leaves," Jefferson said.

"There may be one like it at DeMarco. Go now, would you? Take a few men and some lights. I don't want to wake up in the morning to find out some wino took a crap on it."

Donovan walked back to the body and knelt beside it. He lifted the tarp, picked up the girl's hand, and gently squeezed it. It was cold, like the predawn air. Donovan went home.

BLOODIED BUT STILL IN THERE FIGHTING

Donovan had two suits. One was a brown corduroy he bought at a place that catered to the tweedier types on the West Side. The other he bought downtown, at a small men's shop on Madison Avenue. It was a gray pinstripe which he delighted in telling Jefferson he bought through the mail from a Hong Kong tailor. Everything the sergeant owned came from the highest points of American fashion, and was very expensive. Donovan wore the gray pinstripe for official occasions.

In major cases apt to drag on a bit, Donovan had no peer for impressing reporters. At his first press conference, he showed up in his pinstripe, immaculately groomed, and looking very much the cool professional. At the second, with news worse, he showed up unshaven with his collar open and tie loose. For the third and fourth press conferences, Donovan's appearance gradually deteriorated, until at last he was bleary-eyed and wearing old jeans and dirty basketball sneakers, a huge .44 magnum peeking menacingly from a worn shoulder holster. The overall effect was to give the impression of a department slightly bloodied but still in there trading punches with the enemy.

Flanked by the police commissioner, his press liaison, and a representative of the mayor's office, Donovan gave the reporters just enough information as was prudent. It was enough blood for the most ardent tabloid, but not enough, say, for Dracula. He neglected to mention the kernels of corn or the burnt offerings (which, incidentally, Jefferson *did* find at the DeMarco site). Donovan also left out the ritual aspect of the case, including the halo that had been swept around the victims. He hoped that if any reporters got especially nosey, they would exhaust themselves poking around the public school where both girls went. That connection between the two, he was sure, led no-place.

He was right about the press. No one was especially nosey, and all were content to have the nude bodies of two young girls to wax morbid over. Before Nina Delgado was in the ground, the press would have lost interest entirely.

LET FREEDOM RING

Lois celebrated the arrival of spring by leaving Jack. She moved out of their old apartment in Donovan's building and into a residential hotel on Ninety-sixth Street. She also celebrated by ringing the chimes of some fellow she wouldn't mention by name, but who she assured Donovan was a hot number. Beaming with her newfound freedom, she turned up at Donovan's apartment, bearing determination and a bottle of red Rhône.

"Jack's girl from Iona College is gone. He now has a spic from Ninety-ninth Street," she explained.

"Who also went to Iona College?" Donovan liked to keep his facts straight.

"Not quite. She's a checkout girl at the Grand Union on Eighty-sixth."

"There's lotsa good buys at that store. I got a terrific pepperoni there last week. It was nicely stale and chewy."

"No kidding. Jack got a bargain there, but I don't think he's paying for it. I've stopped giving him money. He got really angry and told me the whole story. He even seemed proud of it. He's been putting the wood to PRs for nearly the whole time we've been married."

"I guess in Ohio, or wherever it is you come from, 'putting the wood to' means 'fucking'?"

"Sure. What else would it mean? And I came from Oregon."

"Does Jack know you're putting the wood to someone?" Donovan asked.

"Damn right. I mean, when I slept with My New Friend for the first time the other night, it was a real revelation. He really *liked* being in bed with me. It wasn't a chore. And he's fun to be with. We actually go places and do things. I can't believe I was faithful to Jack for ten years."

"I can't believe you won't tell me the guy's name," Donovan replied.

"I want to keep it secret for a while."

"Why? Is it someone I know?"

"Bill . . ."

"I know . . . it's Tom Jefferson," he said with a smile.

"Who?"

"My associate, the poor man's Bobby Seale."

"Come *on,*" she laughed. "It's no one you know, and after all the shit I've taken from Jack, I'm entitled to a little intrigue."

"And some revenge as well."

"Absolutely," Lois agreed.

THE WHORE OF BABYLON

Jack went flying to Donovan's apartment complete with beer to cry in, missing his soon-to-be ex-wife by less than an hour.

Donovan put the beer in the ice box and took Jack to Riley's. Lois might come back, and Donovan didn't want his apartment to be ground zero for a marital explosion.

"That cunt has been fucking every guy in town," Jack said, crying instead in a mug of George Kohler's Schmidt's.

"I rather doubt it," Donovan replied.

"She has. I know it. And there I've been breaking my neck finishing my doctorate."

"For only ten years," Donovan mused.

"And she's been running around whoring it up."

"I think I would have heard about it if she was. We talk, you know. She's bent my ear on the subject of your marriage before. That's no secret."

"If she kept it from me, she'd keep it from you," Jack said adamantly.

"Why? If you're gonna air the dirty linen, it makes no point to stop halfway. I think you're wrong."

"I'm not, goddammit!" Jack said, nearly in a shout.

The shout caused George to give a stare into the back room, where Donovan had said he would be entertaining a volatile friend.

"Okay. She's screwing every guy in town. Have it your way."

Jack grinned in relief. Apparently the price of being a reborn bachelor was imagining that Lois drove him to it.

Donovan was not, however, letting him entirely off the hook. "I don't see where you get off being so fucking indignant. What about the Puerto Rican broad who works in the market on Eighty-sixth. Did you think Lois wouldn't tell me how far your Spanish lessons have progressed?"

Jack looked ashamed, and for a moment Donovan was thrilled at his humiliation. The nerve of him, coming around with his popish hypocrisy. Shortly after feeling thrilled, Donovan was as humiliated with his own behavior as Jack was with his. Donovan really wasn't the hard-assed villain he sometimes made himself out to be. Perhaps sensing it, Jack said, "I won't apologize for what I do. She's a wonderful girl . . . beautiful, soft, and understanding. Her name is Sonia."

Donovan shrugged, sipped his beer, and said, "Terrific. Does she have a sister?"

"No, but let me tell you something. If I find out who's fucking my wife, I'm gonna break his goddam neck."

"Don't make death threats in front of cops," Donovan said. "It ain't good business. Besides, necks don't break as easily as you think."

"I was just talking," Jack replied.

HIRED AWAY BY A STEAK & BREW

When Jack was gone, Donovan moved up front to the bar and mumbled raw curses into a glass of Schmidt's.

"Whatsa matter?" George asked, "you lose your ability to solve the problems of the world?"

"I don't need this. On one hand, I got Jack and Lois. On the other hand, I got a case with nothing to go on. Fucking Santa Claus could have jumped out of the bushes and grabbed those kids. I've got men running all over the West Side and still nothing is turning up."

"Why don't you quit your job and go into another line of work?"

"Like what?"

"You could drive a cab?"

"Never. I'd kill the first guy that stiffed me on a tip."

George nodded, then dropped his bomb casually, as if that wasn't what it was. "Then work here," he said.

"What?"

"I need a night bartender."

"What about Mario?"

"He was hired away by a Steak & Brew in Times Square. I'm being serious, Bill. Work nights . . . seven to four. I'll pay you three bills a week and you can pick up a hundred or so in tips. Plus work a little numbers on the side."

"You got to be kidding."

George shrugged. "You spend all your time here anyway."

Donovan couldn't argue that point. Still, he found the offer hard to believe.

"I never tended bar in my life," he said.

"So what? I installed mufflers before I got this job. It ain't all that difficult. You don't get asked to make Singapore Slings. If anybody has the balls to ask, you got the right to tell him where to stuff it. I was in this place on Eighty-fourth one time and a guy came in and asked for a scotch and soda. The bartender told him 'I don't make mixed drinks.' "

Donovan smiled. Forthrightness is to be rewarded. Still, he couldn't imagine himself ending eighteen years in the New York City Police Department to work in a Broadway bar.

"All you have to do is learn a martini, a Manhattan, a Bloody Mary, and the prices. We don't mark the prices on the bottles like some joints, but I'll do it if you want. Most of the time you get asked for beer, shots and beer, and highballs. Nothing you can't figure out in two minutes."

"And of course you wouldn't mind having a bartender who has a gun permit," Donovan said.

"That's no skin off my ass one way or the other. Despite the reputation of this place, we don't have too much trouble. The most trouble we had was one time I had to toss out this customer who was getting on peoples' cases. I go around the bar, right, and he drops into the kung fu position."

"Dachi."

"What?"

"It's called a 'dachi.' So what did you do?"

"Kicked him in the balls," Tom said proudly.

"And it worked? Kung fu is supposed to protect against things like that."

"It didn't in his case. He went out of here on his fuckin' knees and elbows."

Donovan laughed, but shook his head. "Thanks, but I can't take the job right now. Maybe in a couple of years I'll retire, and we can talk about it then."

George seemed unperturbed, to the point where Donovan wondered if the job offer wasn't idle bullshit to begin with. "I got somebody else in mind anyway."

"Who's that?"

"You know her."

"*Her?*"

"Yeah, I'm tryin' to change the image of this place at night. You know how many college kids we got coming in here at night recently?"

Donovan had noticed.

"Well, she should cater to them, and still bring in our old clientele. Rosie is her name . . . you know who I mean."

"I don't."

"Sure you do. Cuban girl. Nice ass. She's been in here."

"I don't know anybody named Rosie," Donovan insisted.

"You'll love her," George said. "Even though she *is* taking your job."

PALM FRONDS?

"Palm fronds?" Donovan exclaimed. "You got to be kidding."

Jefferson shook his head and dropped a plastic evidence bag on Donovan's desk. It was partly filled with black powder in which there were several unburned green specks.

"Just like you mackerel snappers get on Palm Sunday," Jefferson said. "You know, the priest puts some of this black shit on his thumb and sticks it on your forehead."

"And you spend the rest of the day walking around like a goddam maharaja. Only it's Ash Wednesday. If you're gonna insult me, get your facts straight."

Sergeant Jefferson shrugged. "The lab says that the stuff burned at the DeMarco and Delgado sites was palm leaves."

"As if God was anointing the earth, huh?"

"I suppose so."

"Where the hell do you buy palm fronds in this town? Come to think of it, they must be everywhere. There are a lot of Catholic churches. Buy me some, would you? Get a good selection, but the bigger the better."

"Yes, sir. But . . . what do you want them for?"

"What did the killer want them for? I'm gonna put them on my desk and stare at them until a purpose comes to mind. Did you find any Haitian cops?"

"One, but he begged off. He says his family was well off and educated and as a result he doesn't know the slightest thing about voodoo. I'm still looking for others."

"Terrific. Anything else?"

Jefferson seemed a little hesitant, but managed to get it out. "The autopsies showed blood loss," he said, "not consistent with the wounds."

"Meaning?" Donovan asked suspiciously.

"Meaning that approximately one quart of blood was taken from each victim before she died. Apparently through the slash on the wrist."

Donovan whistled between his teeth, something he did almost as well as his loud sigh. "Weirder and weirder."

Jefferson nodded.

"Thank God it wasn't the neck."

"What?"

"Better the wrist. Still, if the press hears about this . . ."

"I'll tell the men to make sure they keep their mouths shut," Jefferson said.

"There was no sign of blood on the ground, so the killer either bottled it or drank it. In either case, he took it with him. What the hell is going on here? Have we come up with anything on cults?"

"Working on it. It's not the sort of thing you stick in a computer. There was that group that chanted over a dead body for a few months some years back, trying to bring it back to life."

"That's crazy, but at least it's the opposite of trying to bring the living to death. Forget them."

"Okay. As far as the West Side goes, there are Moonies on Eighty-sixth and Hare Krishna people on Seventy-second."

"Pains in the ass both, but essentially harmless. That's all?"

"Like I said . . ."

"It's not the sort of thing you find in a computer. So what

we have after two weeks of work is that two girls were abducted while walking on the Riverside Park mall at midevening, taken down into the park and killed as part of a religious rite which may or may not be Caribbean in nature."

"More or less."

"And the fact that both of them were Cuban may also be significant. There were no other important connections between the two. Jesus Christ, I should have taken the job at Riley's after all."

"What?" Jefferson asked, surprised.

FIVE FOOT TWO, EYES OF BLUE

"How does a Cuban get blonde hair and blue eyes?" Donovan asked.

"You have to stand in line a while," Rosalie Rodriguez told him. "But it's a liability. You spend half your life convincing people you're really Cuban."

As the new night bartender at Riley's, Rosie cut a fine figure indeed. The joint needed something to pep it up, and she was perfect. Donovan *did* remember having seen her in the bar as a customer, as George Kohler said he would.

She was a honey, to be sure. Donovan recalled having pondered the notion of trying to pick her up once. Rosie was just over five-feet tall, with light blue eyes and curly blonde hair. She had smallish breasts, but a big, beautiful ass that shook when she walked. Donovan wanted to dive into it head first.

HOT STUFF

"You're a big improvement over Mario, bless his soul," he said. "I hope working in a Steak & Brew suits him."

She shrugged. "Your program is on." She walked down the bar to switch the cable TV from an old Lucille Ball movie to "Rat Patrol." It was three in the morning again, and Donovan was still in his gray pinstripe.

Rosie returned with a brace of beers. She unscrewed the tops and poured some for both of them. "My first day," she said, drinking deeply, "and I can't wait to get out of here."

"Has it been a hard night?"

"The customers were great. I just had no idea how much walking this would involve. My feet are killing me."

"Sore feet are supposed to be *my* problem," Donovan said.

"You don't walk a beat. You're a lieutenant, aren't you? On 'Kojak' being a lieutenant is pretty hot stuff."

"If it wasn't before, it's important now. They've given me twenty extra men and as much money as I need. I feel like a goddam potentate."

If it sounds like Donovan was trying to impress her, he was. She seemed the perfect respite from the fact he was getting nowhere on the case.

"Were those murders as awful as the paper made them seem?" she asked.

"Worse," Donovan said.

She didn't respond. He sensed she was curious, but didn't really want to know all the bloody details.

"I saw you on the news," she said at last, and in a cheery tone of voice. "You looked great . . . a bit like him."

She pointed at the image of Christopher George on television. He was, at the moment, blowing all hell out of a German infantry division.

"Will you marry me?" Donovan said.

"So I said the right thing, huh?" She laughed.

"You did."

"What would happen when you took me home to meet the folks?"

"Nothing. I'll tell them you're not really Cuban. Besides, my family are free spirits."

"I guess we'll have to get married then. Can we do it in the morning, or won't it wait?"

"Morning will be fine. I'm beat to hell too."

"Being on television is tiring?"

"Yeah, though I can't say why. I've done it a few times now, and this one was the worst. I think I'd rather get shot at."

"The lights are hot?"

"More than that, it's the idea of having your brain picked by some clown who looks like he just stepped out of a commercial for designer sunglasses. They're all made up, you know, just spent an hour having their hair styled, and they treat you like you were a three-year-old."

"I still say you looked good."

Donovan smiled, finished his beer, and was given another. The bar was deserted, and closing time less than an hour off. Riley's was on an especially busy stretch of Broadway, which never slept. The bar had a large, plate-glass window that afforded a good view of the activity on the street. There were two fruit and vegetable markets nearby, and three other bars. The markets were open around the clock, and a steady stream of customers poured from the side streets to patronize them. Donovan watched for a while, then went back to the bar and ordered a double shot of Fleischmann's to go with his beer.

"Do you always drink this much?" Rosie asked.

"No. I was just thinking about Nina Delgado. She was the last one killed. Her father was a nice guy, a city bus driver. Someone walked by who looked like her."

Rosie lowered her head and stared at the bar, then sighed. "I feel sorry for the families," she said.

"You can feel sorry for the killer too, 'cause when I catch him I'm gonna hang him by the balls from the highest tree in Riverside Park."

EVEN THE COCKROACHES WERE DOUBLE PARKED

Rosie's apartment was a studio on the top floor of a six-story walkup on Amsterdam Avenue near Ninety-sixth Street. By the time they got to the top floor, Donovan was out of breath.

"I was a lot better at this when I was twenty-five," he said.

"Now you just date girls who live in elevator buildings, right?"

"I make occasional exceptions."

She stopped at her door, turned, took his hand and shook it formally.

"Thanks for walking me home. It's nice to have a police escort."

"It's not a bad idea at this time of night."

"I'd ask you in, but the place is so small . . ."

". . . there's no room for the cockroaches. I know."

"And my sister is staying with me. She's fifteen and will

be here until my parents get back from Miami. They're spending a week with my uncle."

"Don't apologize. It's four-thirty in the morning. Even *I* sleep now and then. Look, I have no idea what your personal life is like; you may be booked up romantically for all I know."

She shook her head.

"But if you can work up any interest in going out with a boring, thirty-eight-year-old cop, I haven't been out in a long time. Maybe I can get theater tickets."

"You got a deal, lieutenant."

LIKE BEING APPROVED OF BY ATTILA THE HUN

Big Harold, the war hero, had taken a liking to Rosie.

It wasn't a *sexual* liking, or didn't seem that way. He just suspended his usual dislike of all who crossed his path for the duration of her tenure as the night bartender.

Harold had never liked anyone before, so no one in the neighborhood knew what form it would take. To the surprise of no one, the form turned out to be practical jokes.

Shortly before midnight, Rosie dashed off to the women's room to rid her body of several beers. Upon her return, she noticed that the assembled had stopped watching a late-night rerun of "Charlie's Angels" and were, instead, watching her. Harold was grinning, an ominous sign.

Rosie had never seen the man smile, and wondered what it meant. She found out when she went to wash a glass and a medium-sized snapping turtle bit her on the hand.

"Christ!" she exploded, yanking her hand away as the bar went up in laughter.

Harold roared, and pounded a fist on the bar hard enough to make glasses jingle.

"What did you put in there? A goddam piranha?"

Harold leaned over the bar and stuck his own hand in the water. The turtle grabbed it, and Harold pulled the creature out, unmindful of the pain, with the turtle dangling from his mammoth paw.

"I bought him for you," he said, slapping the creature on the bar and prying the jaws off the side of his hand. The snapper was sullen and brown, with a ridged shell that made him look like a dinosaur. He stayed where he was put, his mouth open wide enough to reveal a pink tongue, waiting to see if anyone else would be stupid enough to come near.

Rosie said, "You mindless fuck! I ought to toss you the hell out of here!"

"You and what army?" Gillis laughed.

"No wonder Mario went to work for a Steak & Brew. This place is a goddam insane asylum."

Gillis sat back on his stool, leaving Rosie to figure out what to do with the turtle.

"Cook him for your boyfriend," Gillis said, hooking a thumb in the direction of the door. Donovan had just walked in and heard what happened.

Rosie poured herself a scotch and downed it straight off, then cleared her throat with a beer. Donovan was liking her more by the minute. For millennia, men have had drinking buddies and woman friends, and seldom the twain have met. In Rosie, he thought he might have found his perfect woman.

The uproar had quieted, and she seemed to feel better.

"Where the hell did he get a snapping turtle?" Rosie asked.

"The pet shop on Ninety-sixth. I thought of buying him

myself once. I was going to train him to sit on my window-sill and ambush pigeons."

"He's yours," she said quickly, and watched as Donovan picked the thing up by the tail and lowered it into a beer carton.

"I guess Harold and you are friends now," Donovan observed.

"It's kind of like being approved of by Attila the Hun. Still, I must be doing something right. How was your day?"

"Not good, not bad. I managed to finagle tickets to the revival of *On the Town*. If that won't do, I can definitely lay my hands on box seats for the Yanks-Red Sox game."

"Let's go to the theater. I've been to the Bronx enough for a lifetime. Besides, the Yanks aren't gonna beat the Red Sox this early in the season. No way."

"Done," Donovan said happily.

She smiled and patted his hand. "Are you free after closing time? I'm really up for buying a pizza and sitting around talking. For this occasion, I'll let my sister have my apartment to herself. You like pizza, don't you?"

"You bet, but I can't do it tonight," Donovan said, with more reluctance than he could express. "I can't pull another five A.M. bedtime. I have a nine o'clock appointment with the police commissioner to report on progress, and there ain't been much."

"I wish I could help," she said softly.

"Maybe you can. I need a Haitian. Preferably one without too heavy an education."

"What the hell for?" she laughed.

"Just get me one and I'll tell you over pizza. We'll pick up a pizza with everything on it after the theater."

"A Haitian, huh? I've had some odd requests from guys I've dated, but that beats 'em all."

The turtle episode had broken the gloom that had hung over Riley's because of the poor start the Yankees were making in the new season. Little Harold, a gnarled old man of French descent who was hunched over his copy of *The New York Times*, trying without much luck to complete the crossword puzzle, now got lit and took on Wes Jackson, a burly lawyer with a booming laugh that shook the bottles on the backbar. Little Harold jumped to the top of his stool and from there to Jackson's back, howling about how the goddam lawyers, doctors, teachers, businessmen, and ballet dancers who had been buying co-ops along recently upgraded Columbus Avenue were ruining a perfectly good working-class neighborhood. Little Harold started out angry but wound up giggling while Jackson carried him around as if he were a backpack.

Donovan liked Riley's customers. They lived life to the best of their abilities, not doing anything really complicated, but doing it with terrific gusto. For many of them, time at Riley's took up a third of their lives. The saloon was their first stop after work, and the place where they remained until it was time for bed. It was where they came to laugh and forget just how hard they worked to afford living at the center of the known universe.

Donovan was thinking these thoughts and feeling good when Jack came in with his new lover in tow.

DONOVAN'S HEART SANK

Twenty thousand leagues beneath the sea wouldn't be an exaggeration.

The girl may have been soft and understanding, but beautiful was in question. She had a hard face, like someone aspiring to the roller derby, and wore what Jefferson was fond of describing as "spic garb." In this case, it was a purple leotard covered by hot-pink pants belted with an orange and silver scarf, and high-heeled sandals. Her name—Sonia— was on a gold-plated charm hung from a chain around her neck. Her ass was big, which was all that endeared her to Donovan.

Harold spotted her in an instant. "This ain't Times Square," he snapped.

Times Square is one of the prime hooker districts of the Empire City. Jack and Sonia faltered briefly, while uncertainty turned to defiance. Then they went straight to Donovan and took the seats to his left. Rosie walked away to refill some glasses.

"What that guy means is that he's too drunk to know where the hell he is," Donovan said.

Jack smiled forebearingly and made the introductions. Upon being introduced, Sonia squeezed Donovan's thigh. This wasn't a sexual gesture, more like an athlete's pat. Donovan was embarrassed. He took out some papers and began shuffling them, by way of showing he was too busy to talk.

Gloom returned to the barroom. Intruders had embarrassed a regular. Attention shifted back to the television.

Rosie switched the TV to the Mets game starting up on channel nine, and hoped it would cheer things up. The Mets, at least, were winning.

A Spanish-accented man's voice drifted down the bar, saying, "How much it cost, baby?"

Jack didn't blush. Persecution was having its usual effect, hardening the resolve of the victims. Jack needed Lois's leave taking as the excuse to bring Sonia out in the open. Now he needed a small whipping to confirm his new identity. Donovan wished that Jack would take Sonia to the Village—anyplace but *his* bar.

"Your office told me you were here," Jack explained.

Donovan made a silent vow to talk to Jefferson about his big mouth.

"Sonia and I would like to have you over for dinner Saturday," Jack said.

Donovan suppressed a groan. Was he really expected to *socialize* with them? Next, it would be engraved invitations in perfumed envelopes.

"Jack makes great food," Sonia said.

"I know." It was true enough. Donovan had had his veal piccata often, before the couple he identified as Jack and Lois became Jack and Sonia. Somehow, the veal piccata wouldn't taste the same.

"As you can imagine, I've been kind of busy lately," Donovan said. "I'll have to let you know."

He slipped off his barstool and went off in the direction of the head. On the way, he stopped at the other end of the bar, where Big Harold, Wes Jackson, and Rosie were watching Riley's newcomers.

"You guys want to come up with a problem that demands my attention?" he asked. "I need an excuse to stay down this end of the bar."

"I'll throw their asses out," Harold snarled.

"No. Jack's an old friend. I don't want to insult him more than necessary."

"It's a tough life when you can't tell your old friend he's getting to be a pain in the ass," Jackson said.

"Amen to that, brother," Donovan nodded.

"What do they want?" Rosie asked.

"Me to have dinner with them."

"Are you going to do it?"

Donovan shook his head. "There's no way I'd be comfortable. They'd probably be feeling each other up under the table."

"If he's an old friend, you just can't leave him and sit down here," Rosie said.

"You're right," Donovan sighed, and went back.

Sonia had disappeared into the ladies' room. Donovan slid back onto his stool and said, "She seems like a nice girl."

"She's different," Jack said. "She's *natural*. She does what she *feels like*, not what she thinks will impress people."

To be sure, Donovan thought.

"And she's very bright. I know she doesn't have much of a formal education. Just high school."

"One can get by with a high school diploma," Donovan said sharply. Reminded that Donovan himself had never gone to college, Jack blushed and said he was sorry. Donovan said, "Forget it. I never regarded myself as a deep thinker."

"Sonia is special . . . she's a new experience for me." Jack was groping for words, pawing the air as if to grasp one. He said, "She's the first time I've . . . I've . . ."

"Gone to bed with a Puerto Rican girl who's half your age," Donovan said.

Jack was put off, but only for a second. Donovan, he knew, was just getting even for the crack about his lack of education.

"True," Jack said, "but she's Cuban, not Puerto Rican."

"Does it make a difference?"

"My whole adult life I've wanted to know what it would be like to get involved with a girl who doesn't wear plaid skirts and do the Sunday *Times* crossword puzzle with a pen."

"I seem to recall hearing tell of an occasional stewardess," Donovan said.

"Sure, but even they preferred the Philharmonic to punk rock. Sonia likes punk rock. She took me to this place the other night where they . . . well, never mind. You wouldn't be interested."

"Not much, no."

Jack saw Sonia coming back, and said, quickly, "I really like her, William. She's important to me."

"Okay," Donovan said, "tell me what you want me to do."

"Have dinner with us Saturday."

"I can't, Jack. I'm up to my ears in this case. Can it wait a couple of weeks? I may at least have some leads by then."

Jack frowned and, when Sonia returned, wrapped himself up in a passionate kiss.

DONOVAN HAS A REVELATION

"Straps," he said gleefully.

"What?" Jefferson asked.

"Straps. The palm fronds were used for straps."

Donovan held a long one between both hands and tried to break it. He couldn't.

"The girls were tied down hand-and-foot to saplings with the palm fronds. That's how the killer immobilized them while taking their blood. Then he killed them and laid them out where we found them. You remember there were saplings near both murder sites? Check the bark on those trees to see if there's any sign of recent damage."

Jefferson said that he would.

"Palms have significance for Christians. They threw palm fronds at Christ when he rode into town."

"They laid palms at his feet," the sergeant said. "That was Palm Sunday."

"Anointing the ground," Donovan went on. "His timing was a bit off, but we can't have Palm Sundays whenever we need them, can we?"

"*His* timing?"

"Of course. If the girls were tied down, one man could have done it easily enough. He got them to strip at knife point and then tied them up. They probably expected a rape and no more. After he drained the blood and killed them, he burned the palm straps as part of the ceremony."

"I thought we were going on the idea it was a group of people who did it," Jefferson said.

"It still might be. For one person to perform an elaborate human sacrifice on his own seems a little extreme. On the other hand, the very idea of human sacrifice is a mite batty. I was just pointing out it could have been a single killer."

Sergeant Jefferson nodded, and said, "This doesn't have to be a religious thing, you know."

"It's at least partly that in Haiti."

"Are you sure?"

Donovan said, "Find me a Haitian and I'll tell you."

MORE CHICKENS THAN COLONEL SANDERS

For a long time, Donovan had known about the live poultry market on 125th Street, on the western fringe of Harlem. The shop was just down the block from the Twenty-sixth Precinct headquarters. But Rolland Gomez was the only man he knew who had ever set foot in the joint.

"The place has more chickens than Colonel Sanders," Gomez reported. "There's a lot of ducks, geese, and pigeons, too. When you want a bird, you just point out the one and they cut its throat for you."

"Or you can take it for a walk in the park and do the same yourself," Donovan ventured.

"That, too," Gomez said.

Gomez was a handsome Mexican in his fifties whose father was a groundskeeper at the Campo Militar race track outside Mexico City. The family had lived on the grounds, and from this vaguely recalled childhood Gomez had developed a lifelong urge to play the horses as well as a passion for working outdoors. He toiled all day in Riverside Park, picking up garbage and sweeping dog shit into the bushes. He also ran the first aid station at the Ninety-sixth Street tennis courts, and was Donovan's consultant on minor cuts and bruises. Gomez considered horses too sacred a topic for casual discussion. He would, however, discourse gleefully on the subject of the bizarre things people left lying about in the park.

"The other day I picked up four bags full," he said proudly.

"Full of what? Decapitated chickens?"

He nodded. "And pigeons, and all the other stuff they use."

"Such as?"

"Candles. Lots of candles. Some carrots, parsley, and corn, and a cake. I found a cake the other day, in a circle with a dead pigeon and some other stuff."

"What kind of cake? Birthday? Pound? I guess Devil's Food is too obvious a suggestion."

"Birthday," Gomez replied. "Vanilla with lemon icing."

"Was any of it eaten?"

"Not even a little bit. I fed it to the birds. The candles I keep. I like candlelight. The dead pigeons I bury, when I have the time. I try to make the time. People complain, you know. They call up the city and say 'there's a dead goat in Riverside Park and why can't you clean it up? As if we taxpayers don't shell out enough money, etc.' "

"Goat?"

"Last year. They cut the head off, then pulled the body

apart. Two legs were stuck in the ground like tent poles."

Not wanting to hear any more, Rosie walked away, leaving Donovan with Gomez and the Haitian college student she had located. The student's name was Peter Geffrard and, while he was as black as the fabled ace of spades, he spoke English with a fine French accent. He was a good-looking boy, about nineteen, and a student at the Union Theological Seminary, on 120th.

He fingered a glass of Remy Martin nervously. "Haitian voodoo has lost something in moving to New York," he said. "Here you get things like birthday cakes and pigeons. At home, they're a bit more rigorous. Now, I'm not saying I'm an expert . . ."

"Anything you can tell me will help," Donovan said.

"Animal sacrifices are general appeasements to the gods. Mostly it's the god of the growing season. To make the crops better, you know. It goes back to my people's African roots."

"Does this happen only in the spring?" Donovan asked Gomez.

"Year round," he replied, shaking his head and drinking his beer at the same time, not as easy a feat as it sounds.

"Like I said, it's different in New York," Geffrard said. "What seems to be the same is the element of height. The sacrifices are usually on high places . . . hills . . . mountains, if you have them. The high point in the field. And trees. The sacrifice is always at the base of a tree, or on an altar. The spirit of the sacrifice goes up the tree and from there to the god, you see?"

"What about human sacrifices?"

"Not Haitian," Geffrard said quickly.

"You're sure?"

"Positive. In the Americas, the only known human sac-

rifices were Aztec and Pawnee. You can look *that* up, sergeant, it's common knowledge."

"I'm a lieutenant," Donovan said.

"Human sacrifices *aren't* Haitian," Geffrard said again,
with greater emphasis this time.

"Things are different in New York." Donovan shrugged.
Geffrard finished his cognac. "I have to go. I've told you
all I know. To be truthful, lieutenant, I'm uncomfortable
with the subject. It's tough being Haitian on the West Side.
People know what goes on in the park, and they look at you
as if you get your kicks by pulling the heads off chickens and
drinking the blood."

"Drinking the blood?"

"It doesn't happen, but that's what people think. I have
to . . ."

He stopped in mid-sentence. Another black man had
walked in, and was standing by the pinball, looking at him.
Without finishing his drink, Peter Geffrard fled the tavern.
Gomez saw what happened, wisely hunched over his beer
and opened a copy of the *Racing Form*.

The black man went to the bar not far from where Donovan stood and ordered a Bacardi and tonic. Bacardi is sweet,
even for rum, and so is tonic. The combination struck
Donovan as revolting. He went out back to the pay phone
and telephoned his office for a surveillance team. He wanted
the newcomer followed. Geffrard he could always find
again.

When Donovan returned to the bar, the man had finished
his drink and gone. Donovan ran out the door in time to
catch sight of him crossing Eighty-sixth Street and running
south. The man turned east onto Eighty-fifth. By the time
Donovan got to that corner, the street was deserted.

Back at Riley's, Gomez was still picking horses and Rosie

was washing glasses. The bar had filled up some in the two or three minutes Donovan had been gone. He sat down and Rosie gave him back the several dollars and change he had left behind.

"I kept this for you. Never leave money on the bar. What do you think this is, Sardi's?"

"I never had the thought. Where's the glass?"

"You were drinking out of the bottle."

"Not mine, his. The guy I chased out of here."

She held it up, sparkling clean and dripping suds.

"I just washed it. The city makes me do it. The water temperature has to be one hundred and sixty degrees. It's supposed to kill germs, but you and I know it doesn't."

Donovan sighed, and told her about fingerprints. Rosie was unaffected. "I'm not a cop and I don't think like one. If you want me to be a cop, you should deputize me."

"I may yet," he replied.

The next day, Peter Geffrard was gone. After a day's phone calls, all Donovan's men were told was that he had taken the first flight back to Haiti, where his father was a minor official in the government of Jean-Claude "Baby Doc" Duvalier.

INVISIBLE

The man who had so frightened Geffrard was, though black, quite invisible. Haitian blacks are hard to distinguish from any other blacks until they open their mouths and start spouting French accents. Rosie and George thought they had seen him in the bar. But bartenders usually identify customers whose names they don't know by the times of day they come in and what they drink. Unfortunately, Bacardi and tonic wasn't as unusual a thing to order as Donovan thought. He consoled himself with the knowledge that Pancho and his technicians had found traces of palm fronds on six of the eight saplings to which the two victims might have been tethered. That meant the killer could have been either singular or plural, or one masquerading as the other.

ROSIE LOOKS GOOD

On the Town proved worthy. Donovan didn't get to Broadway shows often, and when he did he leaned toward the "name" shows—*A Chorus Line, Sleuth, Company, Evita, 6 Rms Riv Vu, Death Trap,* and, going back awhile, *West Side Story,* and *The King and I.* He liked musicals, although he did make it to the first run of *Who's Afraid of Virginia Woolf* because people screaming at one another reminded him of his job.

Afterward, he and Rosie bought pizza and a bottle of chablis that Donovan's wine merchant assured him was a bargain at fifteen dollars. They ate in Donovan's apartment by the window in the dining room. Rosie wore a black dress, carried a gold purse, and looked fabulous.

When the meal was over, they drank Benedictine and watched a tug pull coal barges down the Hudson. He had cleaned up his apartment for the occasion, and it looked only vaguely like a meeting between a tornado and a beer hall. She took his arm and wrapped it around her, nestling against his side.

The park was dark and quiet-looking, with only the periodic dots of the electric lamps to break the darkness. Headlamps sped rapidly up and down the West Side Highway and, across the Hudson, New Jersey cars seemed to crawl along the riverbank.

"I'm sorry I washed that glass," she said. "I promise to be more careful from now on. The next time a murderer comes into my bar, I won't touch a thing."

"Ah, forget it. The guy was probably Geffrard's pimp. Or his dope dealer. That's it, his dope dealer. The dealer smelled a bust and split. There . . . you have my instant analysis of what happened."

She smiled, took his hand, and intertwined his fingers with hers. "You have a funny way about you for a cop. I mean, you don't seem coplike. Does that make sense?"

"Sure it does. My captain tells me the same thing. It may be that I've never beaten up a suspect. I don't like coplike cops. After a while, they end up 'ten-fouring' everyone and can't seem to get a sentence out without telling everyone how tough they are."

"I like your way better."

"By the same token, you don't seem very much like a Cuban chick who works in a Broadway bar," he said.

"It's the blue eyes, like I told you." She laughed, and turned toward him. "How's this . . . 'hey meester, que pasa?' "

"Nada," he shrugged.

"Oh yeah?" She snaked her arms around his neck and pulled his head down to hers.

FOND

"I could get fond of you," Donovan said, lying on his back and feeling the cool breeze coming off the river.

Rosie gave his balls an affectionate squeeze by way of letting him know she appreciated the thought. She liked to sleep with her hand on his private parts, as if to let them go would be to give them up forever.

Donovan and Rosie had dozed off after making love. She was sensational, as he knew she would be. Her ass was even lovelier up close. Donovan had, as he wanted, dived in head first.

"How can you stand living alone in this great big apartment?"

"I fill it up with garbage. Old newspapers, beer cans . . . you know. That way it doesn't seem so big."

"It's criminal for one man to live alone in an apartment this size. How many rooms *are* there? I lost count."

"Three bedrooms, three baths. Living room, dining room, kitchen, and foyer."

"Criminal, like I said. You ought to arrest yourself."

"Look, the place has been in the family two generations now. I pay under four hundred bucks a month for this. The day I vacate the premises, it goes off rent control and the rent doubles. So, you see I can't leave. Keeping this apartment is striking a blow for tenants' rights."

"Umf," she said.

"The landlord would love to get me out. But he can't pull the usual shit—cutting off the heat and hot water and stuff like that—because I'm a cop."

Donovan rolled toward her and ran a hand lightly over her breasts. "You don't have to go home tonight, do you?"

She said that she didn't, and answered the caress with some of her own. They made love again, then lit cigarettes and blew smoke at the ceiling.

"What about your sister?" he asked.

"What about her?"

"Will she be all right alone?"

"She's not alone. My parents are back from Miami, so she's home with them on Amsterdam. They have a place right across from the post office. Besides," Rosie laughed, "my sister does okay anyway."

He asked what she meant.

"She has a boyfriend who treats her royally. He and his friends act like she's some kind of princess."

"If she's like you, she deserves it."

"Cheap flattery," Rosie said, "but I'll take it."

DAWN PATROL

Donovan answered the door wearing an old pair of jeans and nothing else. His apartment still smelled of pizza, wine, and cigarettes. Donovan wasn't hung over; he had been too busy making love to get drunk the night before. Still, he gave Sgt. Thomas Lincoln Jefferson a baleful stare.

"We take deliveries at the servants' entrance," Donovan snarled.

Jefferson was unmoved. "The Coast Guard picked up a floater a couple of hours ago off the nude sunbathing pier at Seventy-first Street. Had two slugs in the back of his head. Peter Geffrard. I guess the prick missed his plane."

WHO THE HELL USES AN INNER TUBE ANYMORE?

The Port Authority cop guarding the pier to which the Coast Guard brought the remains of Peter Geffrard was a little man, deeply tanned from years of watching shit float by on the Hudson, and not of a mind to be surprised by anything, let alone the bodies of black men.

"Who *is* this guy, lieutenant?" he asked.

"A lonely passenger on the river of life," Donovan said, without conviction. It was early in the morning.

"Lots of stuff floats down this river," the man went on. "I seen lots of stiffs. Of course," he laughed, "they ain't so stiff once they've been in the water a while. You grab 'em by the hair and the head falls off. Dead fish, too. Millions of 'em. Every couple of months a great big school of dead fish washes by. I don't know what kind of fish they are. They look like snapper blues to me, only they're too big. Anyway, each one has a big bite taken out of it. The head and a bit past the gills is missin'. Whatever it was that ate 'em ate the part nobody usually wants."

"These is unusual times," Donovan replied.

"Railroad ties . . . oil barrels . . . sunken row boats . . . and inner tubes! You tell me who the hell has an inner tube anymore."

The Hudson smelled of human feces and machine oil. The city was still too broke to finish the North River Pollution Plant, and as a result the West Side was emptying its toilets straight into the river. After a night of incredible romance, it was too much for Donovan's soul. He turned away from the river and, putting a comradely hand on Jefferson's shoulder, walked to the spot where Geffrard's body lay a-moulderin' in the morning sun.

"Someday all this will be yours," he said.

"Thanks a lot, lieutenant."

OVERKILL

"The second bullet was overkill," Donovan said, turning away from the body as he turned away from the river.

Jefferson nodded. "There can't have been too much left to put a slug in. It's kinda like shootin' Jell-o, if you know what I mean."

"Take a guess at the sequence of events," Donovan said.

"Shot. Dumped in river," the sergeant said.

"On the way to the airport? What was in his pockets?"

"His wallet, containing the usual shit and a little under three bills."

"That's a lot of walking around money for a theology student to have on him," Donovan said.

"No foolin'."

"What about the trappings of travel? A passport, for example? Or airline tickets?"

"Nope. I got his apartment keys, though. You wanna go up there?"

"Where's he live?"

"International House. Up by Columbia."

"I know. Yeah, let's go see his apartment."

They walked across the gravel and dust of the abandoned pier to where their car was waiting. As Jefferson drove north on the West Side Highway en route to the heights, he said, "You think this has something to do with the Haitian angle on our two murders?"

"No. I think he bought a bad bottle of Ripple and it blew up in his face."

"Hey," Jefferson protested, "don't play Heavy Honkie with *me*. Just because I took you away from your little muchacha."

"Watch it, boy . . ."

"I know, you'll have me walking a beat."

"No, I'se gonna have you back pickin' cotton."

"You can't fire me. I'm black. That makes me privileged. You try to fire me and you got the N-double-A-fuckin' C-P down on your head in ten seconds."

"Just drive the car and shut up," Donovan said, leaning his head back, yawning, and closing his eyes.

Jefferson laughed. "Yeah, and you just sit there and pick Puerto Rican hair outta your teeth."

"She's Cuban," Donovan replied, and looked out the window as the sun rose above the tall old buildings on Riverside Drive.

MARSH RECLAMATION

Geffrard's apartment was dirtier than Donovan's. It looked like the soft underbelly of a sanitary landfill site.

"What's cleanliness close to?" Jefferson asked. "Godliness?"

"Impossible," Donovan replied.

"This place has been tossed over," the sergeant went on. "Do tell."

It was a classic case of an apartment being turned inside out. Geffrard's apartment was a large studio with a kitchenette. That is to say, a cubby-hole into which was crammed a half-pint ice box, a two-burner stove, and a tiny sink. The walls were decorated with a Miró print, a very early Picasso, and several photographs showing Haitian dignitaries. The last-mentioned were presented without captions, but one recurring figure in a clean white linen suit appeared to be Geffrard's father, caught in the act of shaking hands with various Haitian military figures.

Four brown-suited detectives went through the rubble while their superiors watched. Every piece was examined— the drawers turned upside down, the books cast onto the floor, the personal papers carefully scrutinized. When it was done and the four detectives had given their reports, Jefferson consulted his clipboard and took a deep breath.

"Everything's here that should be here," he said.

"Passport? Airline tickets?"

"Both. And handwritten notes saying that Aunt So-and-So will meet him at the airport. He was supposed to arrive yesterday."

"No problems making decisions, this boy," Donovan said.

"None. He was goin', all right. But he got stopped."

"Is there anything here that has him belonging to any Haitian groups?" Donovan asked. *"Anything* relating to the case. You know what I want."

Jefferson shook his head. "We got an address book, but at first glance there doesn't seem to be anything out of the ordinary. A couple Columbia numbers. A couple broads. Riley's . . ."

"Riley's?" Donovan asked.

"Yeah, that shithole you drink at. What of it?"

"I spend a good deal of my life in there, and I don't recall seeing Geffrard before. Look, Pancho, *I* don't even know the phone number of the place, and I think I'm in love with the bartender. Why would he write down Riley's phone?"

"Maybe he was tryin' to hit on your chick."

"She hasn't been there that long. Besides, she doesn't go for spades, and I can't blame her."

"Geffrard wasn't a spade! Now wait a minute . . ."

"Control yourself, son. I don't have the time or patience to sort out the internecine rivalries of the world's nonwhites. You don't like Spics? Terrific. Just spare me the details, especially since I'm falling for one."

Jefferson calmed down, then smiled. *"You* figure out why he wrote down Riley's phone number. I got all the rest of this junk to go through. You wanna go home now?"

"You bet. I got to stop at Zabar's and pick up breakfast first, though."

"Whatsa matter, lieutenant?" Jefferson asked, a look of vengeful glee in his eyes, "Your Chiquita Banana can't cook too good?"

BUT SHE COULD COOK

And did. Within half an hour of Donovan's return, she had whipped up an array of corn muffins, scrambled eggs, and bacon. They ate on a card table set up by the living room window. From the fifteenth floor of a Riverside Drive apartment, it was impossible to particularize the shit floating down the Hudson. The view was lovely. So was Rosie, dressed as she was in one of Donovan's white shirts.

"That's awful about Gef . . . what was his name?"

"Geffrard," Donovan said, "and it may not have been awful."

"What do you mean?"

"Geffrard was a bad guy. Just how bad, and in what line of work, remains to be determined. Nobody gets two in the back of the skull without deserving it in one way or the other. He obviously was running away from someone, either me or one of his confederates. He didn't make it. As the saying goes, 'tough shit.' "

"Why do you say he might have been running away from you?" she asked.

"Okay, Geffrard was heavily into something illegal . . ."

"You don't think he's the one who killed those two girls?"

"It could be. So all of a sudden this cop comes into his life, asking questions. That's enough to bring out anyone's paranoia. Do you realize that ninety-nine percent of the people in the world go through their lives without ever being asked a question by a cop? Let alone questions about such dainty matters as human sacrifice."

"I guess that could be unsettling," she allowed.

"It could put you right off your feed, especially if you *were* involved in human sacrifice. So Geffrard decides to fly the coop but his associates, whoever they may be, don't want to trust him to keep his mouth shut in the event he's caught. And they have to assume he will be caught. He's a foreign student in New York, and the son of a government official in Haiti. He can't exactly drop out of sight and get a job washing dishes in some greasy spoon in the Bronx."

Rosie nodded, and pushed another muffin toward Donovan, who was already stuffed.

"I can't believe I've been pouring drinks for the man who killed those two girls," she said.

"Whether or not that was the case remains to be seen," Donovan said, buttering the muffin and taking a bite out of it.

"Why," she asked, "did he have Riley's phone number in his book?"

"Assuming George and you don't know him, there's only one explanation. He routinely contacted his partners-in-crime there."

"Do you mean I may be serving *more* of them?" she gasped.

"I doubt that the one I chased off will be back, but there may be others. If Geffrard just wanted to contact one guy, he could have made simpler arrangements. No, I would say it's pretty definite you'll be serving Geffrard's accomplices."

"Jesus Christ, William!"

"Stay behind the bar and you'll be safe. Look, darling, Geffrard still could have been into dope. This still could have nothing to do with the murders. In fact, I'd say it's odds-on that Geffrard had nothing to do with the murders. If he had, he wouldn't have been willing to talk to me about them. I don't know that many people who are into human sacrifice, but my guess would be they're sufficiently up tight not to want to discuss it at *all.*"

Rosie seemed partly mollified.

"Just the same," Donovan went on, "if anyone comes in with black skin and a French accent, I want you to refrain from washing anything he touches. Why take chances?"

"Yeah, and one other thing."

"Oh?"

"I want you there every second I'm on the job. Look at it this way . . . I'm offering you an excuse to spend eight hours a day in a bar. You can tell the commissioner it's a stakeout."

The police commissioner was unmoved by the argument.

"You remember that time Lieutenant DiGioia and Sergeant Culmone absolutely . . . positively, had to spend two months in a whorehouse as part of an investigation?"

"No," Donovan replied.

"So now you tell me you have to spend an indefinite amount of time in an Irish bar on the West Side."

"It only appears to be an Irish bar. It's owned by Jews and patronized by Hispanics, principally Cubans."

The commissioner thought a moment. "Could this be a Cuban thing and not a Haitian thing? The two victims *were* Cuban."

"I'm not sure that it's either," Donovan said. "It's easy to call it a Haitian ritual because it *was* a ritual and the Haitians *do* have rituals in Riverside Park. It's easy to call it a Cuban thing because the two victims *were* Cuban. On the other hand, it could have to do with P.S. 487. In short, who the hell knows? I'm trying to investigate the leads I have and otherwise keep my options open."

The commissioner thought for a longer moment.

"What about the Haitian kid you pulled out of the river?"

"*I* didn't pull him out. I was otherwise engaged the night he was killed. Like I said in my report, it might not have anything to do with the two girls' deaths."

"I know what you *wrote*. What do you *think?*"

"I think I'm gonna keep my options open and spend a lot of time at Riley's," Donovan said.

"You really believe it all revolves around that gin mill, don't you?"

"I do."

"Why?"

"Riley's is a melting pot for your Broadway blue-collar guys and the posher sorts from Columbus Avenue. I got my Haitian stuff there, and Geffrard wrote the phone number in his address book. The place is the key to it all. Believe me one more time, won't you?"

"Okay," the commissioner said, "although in my heart of hearts I suspect this is one more case of a cop having to spend two months in a whorehouse."

"KILL THAT SUCKER," THEY SHOUTED

What Donovan liked to call "a good old West Side blow-out" started at Broadway and Eighty-ninth a little after eight o'clock. Two young black men all spiffed up for a night on Forty-second Street were showing off their beige El Dorado to the older and very tired black men sitting outside a welfare hotel. The young men did it by driving by slowly several times, gunning the engine, and sending volumes of gray smog out of the chrome exhausts and onto their elders.

Now, their elders were drinking Colt 45 out of the can and it was a hot night; their patience was far from inexhaustible. They were about to suggest that the boys in the Caddy take their business elsewhere when half-a-dozen Puerto Ricans in a beat-up old Chevy came careening down Broadway and sideswiped the El Dorado.

The fight was short but glorious. As the elders of the welfare hotel watched in delight, the Ricans whomped the shit out of the blacks. It took four squad cars from the Twenty-fourth Precinct and half of the West Side Major Crimes Unit to break it up. The crowd scene at the corner of Eighty-ninth was admirable. Taking vague interest in the matter, Donovan, now in jeans and sneakers, drifted out of Riley's, a bottle of Schmidt's in his hand. Jefferson, the ranking cop on the scene (for Donovan was pretending he wasn't a cop), was gentlemanly. He decided to write off the whole thing and send everyone on his way. It was forgiveness all around. That is, until the cops left.

As soon as they were gone, the blacks in the Caddy took after the Ricans in the Chevy, who were stopped for the light at Eighty-sixth. There, the fight started anew. Incensed at having the show leave on a road trip without consulting them, the elders of the welfare hotel ran down Broadway to watch. Donovan was right with them.

As the chief black fought it out with the principal Rican, patrol cars descended on the scene from all directions. More than nine of them showed up this time, and Jefferson was madder than hell. As Donovan drank and watched, Jefferson got the leaders of the fight, had them stretched across the hoods of their respective cars, and proceeded to whomp the shit out of them, but properly. Two white couples who had drifted over from a nouvelle cuisine dinner on Columbus Avenue stood in the crowd, clucking their tongues while two white cops held the black man down and Jefferson banged his head against the hood of the El Dorado, making a fine dent. The white couples looked to the elders of the welfare hotel, expecting them to join in disapproval of such blatant police brutality.

The couples were to be disappointed. "Kill that sucker," the welfare guys shouted at the cops.

When things calmed down, Donovan sauntered over to where Jefferson stood, fingering his bruised knuckles.

"Striking a few blows for righteousness, huh?" Donovan asked, sipping his beer.

"Cheap niggers like this give us all a bad name," Jefferson

replied. "I tell you, Bill, it's getting harder and harder to keep one's dignity in this city."

BIG HAROLD WILL PUNCH HIS TICKET

"He's still at it," Lois moaned.

"What now?"

"You didn't have dinner with Sonia and Jack Saturday. He's accusing me of having stolen your friendship. Now you're *my* friend and not *his*. He thinks I deliberately turned you against him."

"Why is this happening to me?" Donovan lamented.

"It's because you're the only one he has to talk to. He can't bring Sonia to Grad Facs beer parties. He'd be laughed out of the doctoral program. He's only got you and his shrink to lean on, and you're cheaper. The shrink costs forty dollars a session. You'll listen to him for the price of a bottle of beer."

"I think I'll get my war hero friend to punch his ticket after all."

"Have him punch it once for me," Lois said. "You know what Jack has been doing? I mean, aside from calling my parents and telling them what a whore I am . . ."

"Has he been doing that?"

"Yeah, and at four in the morning, just to make sure they pay attention. He told them the other night he has evidence I've been sleeping with at least a dozen guys."

"I'd like to see the evidence. No, on second thought, I wouldn't. Just keep me in mind if you decide to expand the list."

"I thought you didn't like redheads. Anyway, Jack really

wants me to pay him alimony, or at least keep picking up the bill for his shrink. He says I made him nuts."

Donovan shook his head sadly, but as the gesture couldn't be seen over the phone, Lois asked him what he thought.

"Stop paying for his shrink and invest the money in a lawyer. Jack's not your responsibility, and whatever he does isn't your fault. I have to go. Rosie goes on duty in an hour, and she won't work unless I'm there."

"I can't believe you've finally found a girl," Lois laughed.

"I've had girls before."

"Yeah, but . . . you know. A barmaid! I think it's terrific."

"Don't patronize me, Lois," Donovan said. "I'm too old to suffer the forebearance of my friends. If you don't like my seeing Rosalie Rodriguez . . ."

"Touchy . . . aren't we?"

"Yeah," Donovan sighed, "I guess we are."

DIVE! DIVE! DIVE!

Little Harold was a legend in the defense industry.

He had spent the final years of his long and fruitful career working in the shipyard in New London, Connecticut, building Trident submarines for the Navy. There he would always be remembered as the hero of the Great Ivory Soap Rescue.

Little Harold was an interior wiring specialist, which is what he claimed men of his stature do when they don't ride race horses. Because of his diminutive stance—four-foot-ten at best—he was able to crawl inside the submarine's electrical and air ducts. Once inside, it was his job to install the millions of wires needed to run the myriad systems of America's first aquatic line of nuclear defense. Little Harold also tested the bridge wiring, and was one of the very few people in the world who knew how to launch a pre-emptive nuclear strike. He used this amazing information whenever he was accused of being just another illiterate West Side drunk.

During the 1970s, because of pressure from women's groups, General Dynamics hired three female interior wiring specialists to complement the eight men already on the job. This was fine with Little Harold, who liked women even better than he liked booze. But there was a snag. Little Harold's last week before retirement coincided with the women's first week. One of them crawled inside the port air refiltration system of a Trident, got a few dozen yards down the tube, and was stuck fast at the hips. A woman's hips, as evolutionists, fashion designers, and dirty old men will tell you, are proportionately wider than a man's.

The female specialist, caught fast inside the air system, became hysterical. Her body swelled. It took Little Harold two hours to calm her down and six hours to get her out. The rescue involved his cutting off every stitch of her clothing and soaping her from head to foot with a bar of Ivory Soap. During those six hours, Little Harold saw more pussy than in all the previous years of his life. He retired a happy and fulfilled man, and the girl was reassigned to exterior maintenance.

Little Harold told his story whenever he could. That wasn't often, for he was generally avoided. He'd grown crabby with age, and was apt to leap to a barstool and from there to someone's back, a gnarled old vampire, if he didn't like the way the conversation was going. But now and then, his eyes would turn kindly, he'd buy the listener a drink and tell the story of the Great Ivory Soap Rescue one more time.

MISTAKING EXHAUSTION FOR BOREDOM

"He's driving me crazy," Sonia said.

Donovan was happy that apart from Rosie and Little Harold, who was drunk, no one else was in the bar at the time.

"I don't know what he *wants.*"

"Neither do I, and I'm not sure I care anymore."

Sonia took the gesture of sympathy as an invitation to explain herself. In short, in becoming a late-in-life Lothario, Jack had found that the single life wasn't what he expected.

All those orgiastic nights filled with titter, wine, and semen turned out to be merely exhausting. Not willing to admit to his increasing age, Jack mistook exhaustion for boredom. The lack of excitement turned out to be Sonia's fault. He wanted new horizons.

Sonia couldn't cure Jack, whose need had become insatiable.

"He's into little girls," she said.

"How little?" Donovan asked.

"Fifteen or sixteen."

"Cubans?"

"Yeah. He says he likes our skin tone."

"I can understand that much at least. What am I supposed to do about this?"

"You know him better than I do," she went on. "I think he's cracking up, and I don't know what to do about it."

"I think he's cracking up, too, and I'm no more of a shrink than you are. What the hell do you expect me to do? You're the one who's sleeping with him, for Christ's sake."

"Not any more."

Donovan elevated his eyebrows. "You're leaving him?"

"My bags are packed."

"My God, in a month, the son of a bitch has been run out on by the WASP he loves and the Cuban he loves. What's next?"

"Who knows?" Sonia replied. "Who cares?"

DONOVAN IS MADE TO FEEL OLD

Rosie's parents served arroz con pollo the way it should be —with both red and green peppers, peas, and asparagus tips. There was a good Spanish wine for the women and beer for the men, and sexual segregation for much of the afternoon. The women kept to the kitchen and dining room, and the men huddled around the TV, watching the first Yankee game of the season.

Santos Rodriguez was a muscular, passionate man of fifty or so, the foreman of a repair gang on the subway tracks. His wife, a small woman who seldom spoke, gave the impression of having devoted her life to raising beautiful daughters. Rosie's fifteen-year-old sister Camelia was nothing short of a beauty. She had soft brown hair and eyes to match, and a lithe figure well-suited to her main avocation, playing tennis.

Donovan didn't know much about tennis, but Johnny Silver Shoes, Camelia's mentor, did. He was a Columbia sophomore, nineteen years old, and said to be an up-and-coming tennis player. Silver Shoes had narrowly missed being selected for the Junior Davis Cup team, and was a local luminary on the Riverside Park courts. An American Indian, he looked noble enough to belong on a nickel. Camelia was his tennis protégé, and the darling of his friends.

Donovan was grateful for Johnny's presence at the Rodriguez apartment that Sunday afternoon. He couldn't figure the relationship between Johnny and Camelia—it didn't appear to be sexual—but he was glad that Johnny and Camelia, not Rosie and he, were the main focus. Being brought home to meet Rosie's parents made him feel old, even ancient. At thirty eight, he was twelve years older than Rosie, and *she* was taunted by her mother for being a spinster. Donovan regarded himself as her father's contemporary more than hers, and Camelia struck him as still in diapers.

"I'm too old for this," he told Rosie afterward. "If I decide to marry you, do I have to ask their permission?"

"Absolutely," she replied. "But don't worry about it. I don't want to marry an old man."

Back at his apartment, Donovan cracked a can of Budweiser and stood by the bedroom window, watching the dozens of antlike figures scurrying around the Ninety-sixth Street tennis courts.

Rosie showered, then appeared by his side, towelling herself off.

"My parents like you," she said.

"He's down there."

"What?"

"I can feel it."

"Who?" she asked, looking down at the busy Sunday park. "What?"

"Him. Or them. It could be one or the other. But I know he's there. He might even be looking up at me."

"You're a dreamer, William. He's probably gone away and will never be heard from again."

"Now who's the dreamer?" he replied.

Rosie handed him the towel. "Dry my back," she said.

Beneath the city of New York was a shadow city, dark and dripping water, walls moist with algae. Rats ducked in and out of the shadows, where huge conduits carried drinking water to buildings and sewage away from them. Vast networks of underground channels held electrical and phone cables, and the access room for repairmen. There were water mains, subways, and tunnels for railroad tracks leading out of town.

Hobos and blind rats live under Grand Central Station in conduits designed for workmen but seldom used by them. Below Riverside Park, through gigantic, six-foot pipes laid for the shelved North River Pollution Plant, a dark, hulking figure walked slowly.

There were people he had to see, things he had to do.

Beneath Riverside Park, beneath even the railroad tracks, the never-used sewer conduit led to a square, concrete room which was to have been a pumping station. Now it was nothing, caught forty feet below ground, forgotten even by its designers, separated from the lowest level of the multi-level park by a steel door set into a concrete abutment. The external face of that door was overgrown with vines and graffiti. A rusted lock gave the appearance of never having been used. Few park employees knew what lay behind that door, but most assumed it was just another unused access to the railroad tracks.

The man who had come so far to reach that room paused in it. The floor was fastidiously clean, swept even of dust. Outside, dusk was half an hour away. He set a candle in a brass holder and placed it in the center of the room. He lit the candle, and shut off his flashlight once the room was bathed in the candle's flickering light. The incessant traffic on the West Side Highway caused deep, low vibrations which reminded him of the drone of high-power electric motors. A rat squeaked. The man jumped to his feet, but without making noise, and cocked an ear in the direction of the sound.

The rat didn't repeat itself, and the man settled back down, though his nerves were still on edge. He heard silence, ancient echoes, electronic beeps which might have been more rats. The sun would soon set, and he would be free again. He took out the key to the lock which would bring him yet again to the surface of Riverside Park.

BIG ENOUGH FOR HALF OF HAVANA

"This place is big enough for half of Havana," Camelia said, sweeping her tennis racket around Donovan's living room.

"I know." Rosie brandished a broom and was trying to clean up the beer cans, cigarette butts, and old copies of *Sports Illustrated* littering the floor.

Camelia was on her way to a late afternoon lesson at the Ninety-sixth Street courts. She had stopped at Donovan's apartment to see the place where her sister had been spending so much time. Rosie's sudden fondness for Donovan

struck Camelia as fascinating. Rosie had always seemed im-
mune to permanent attachments. Donovan fascinated Camelia too. She had never known a cop, let alone one from an
old West Side family with an apartment that seemed to go
on forever. On Amsterdam Avenue where the Rodriguez
family lived, such an apartment would be occupied by eighteen people, not by a solitary, eccentric cop.

"It's gonna take you a week to clean up this place," Camelia observed.

"Or a year," Rosie said, filling yet another plastic garbage
bag and twisting the top closed.

"You really love him, don't you?"

"I don't know." Rosie blushed a little.

"Come on . . . you do."

"I've only been going out with him a couple of weeks."

"So what? You're living with him."

"I'm not."

Camelia laughed. "Your clothes are in his closet. Your
makeup is in the bathroom."

"He has a dozen closets and three bathrooms," Rosie said.
"I keep some stuff here in case I need it."

"Which seems to be all the time," Camelia said.

"I spend time at my apartment."

"Sure. Can I have your apartment when you marry him?"

"I'm not marrying him," Rosie said quickly.

"When you move in with him, then. I got to get off
Amsterdam."

"You're too young to have your own apartment," Rosie
said.

"I'm nearly sixteen."

"Like I said, you're too young. And what do you want
to leave home for? Johnny?"

"And why not? Johnny's beautiful. And he's so good to me."

Rosie sighed. "You're a child, and I don't give children advice about men. Go and play tennis. I want to have the bedroom done before he gets home."

"Where is he?"

"Out working. How the hell do I know? Are you meeting Johnny?"

"Sure. He's working on my top spin."

"And a good deal more than that, probably."

"Johnny is the perfect gentleman," Camelia said.

Rosie went back to sweeping. There was an old box of Wheat Thins under the bed, along with a brown and a blue sock and a much-abused softball bat.

Camelia peered out the window at the tennis courts. Donovan's apartment was on the northwest corner of the building, and the bedroom faced both north and west. The courts and, beyond them, the river north to the George Washington Bridge were etched by the late day sun.

"I'd love to live here," Camelia said. "I could keep track of Johnny no matter what he did. Look at this view!"

"Look at the garbage," Rosie replied, looking at the box of Wheat Thins with incredible distaste.

A CASE OF TENNIS BALLS

When Rolland Gomez wasn't picking up garbage in the park, he watched the tennis courts. The latter was by far the preferred activity. Watching the tennis courts involved sitting in the little concrete bunker next to the playing area, drinking beer, and bullshitting with his friends.

The bunker had a locker room and an office, and a refrigerator in which a copious supply of beer was maintained. There was a small TV on which to watch ball games, and no end of friends with whom to bullshit. "This is my country club," Gomez liked to say, as he handed out bottles of George Kohler's Schmidt's and watched aspiring young Borgs and McEnroes working up sweats. On hot summer days, there was a procession of drunks from Riley's, where the air conditioner was typically out of order, to Gomez's country club, where a fine breeze blew in off the Hudson.

Donovan occasionally visited that club. He liked to be on hand as the wizened old men from Riley's watched the young tennis bucks trying to impress one another with forehands and backhands that would cut little ice with Borg and McEnroe. Donovan found the scene amusing. It would have been good had he been able to visit the country club that day.

SILVER SHOES IS A NO-SHOW

It wasn't the first time Silver Shoes stood Camelia up, but it was quite definitely the last. After waiting an hour at the courts, Camelia drifted into the bunker, where Gomez was lounging with his feet up. His work day was over, and he was watching an old episode of "Ironside."

"Hi," she said, "have you seen Johnny?"

He shook his head. "Not today. Is he supposed to be here?"

"A while ago."

"He didn't sign up for a court. Do you have a partner?"

"No."

"What can I say? You want a court?"

It was her turn to shake her head. "I'll wait a while longer."

"There's not too many signed up. You can work on your serve."

"No, thanks," she said. "If he doesn't show in a little while, I'll go home. Thanks anyway."

"So long," Gomez replied, not calling her by name, for he couldn't remember her name. Like bartenders, tennis court attendants have their own way of identifying customers: type of racket, time of day they were most likely to show up. To Gomez, Camelia was "the Spanish girl with the Evert who comes late in the day."

Camelia waited for Johnny Silver Shoes until she could wait no longer. Then she tucked her racket under her arm and stormed away from the courts. Camelia was angry at having been stood up, and needed something to take it out on. She picked the handball courts at 79th Street. A half hour of whacking a tennis ball against the concrete wall should do the trick, she thought.

Camelia made for the handball courts, unmindful of the approaching darkness or the danger lurking in the caverns beneath her feet.

JOE HALFTRACK

Donovan had for years avoided the man generally known as Joe Halftrack, and not without reason.

The stark-bald man of sixty or so was conceivably the biggest pain in the ass on the West Side. There were a lot of really annoying characters on Broadway, but Halftrack topped them all because he worked at it. Being a pain in the ass was a source of pride to him. He practiced his art with all the diligence of an athlete training for the Olympics.

His style was simple and effective. He stood in bars (or, when no bars would serve him) on street corners, insulting people. To this timeless technique he added a novel twist— partial paralysis. He knew that no one would punch out a guy in an orthopedic walker.

Halftrack's standard aluminum walker was modified with assorted plastic and canvas bags that he had meticulously wired to the struts. The man carried all his possessions with him, dangling from the metal superstructure. He had no other home. Among his possessions were myriad metal and glass objects, so his arrival was accompanied by a great deal of clanking and jangling. He sounded like a gypsy caravan and resembled a small armored vehicle, and his arrival nearly always resulted in a fight.

When simple insults weren't enough, Halftrack would start fights between others. A favorite line: "Are you really a fag? That guy down the bar says so." When such tactics didn't work, he generally resorted to direct violence. He'd toddle up to a man sitting on a barstool, brace his frame, then grab the man by the neck and yank, toppling his victim.

Halftrack had acquired his infirmity and his nickname some decades earlier, when he failed to live up to an obligation to a Broadway loan shark. The shark took Halftrack to the Jersey pine barrens and drove a car over his back. The car was a 1962 Chevette, a compact, so Halftrack stayed alive. "It should have been a fuckin' tank," George Kohler said often.

Halftrack had, at one time or another, been eighty-sixed at every bar on Broadway. One gin joint even narrowed the width of the front door so he couldn't get his walker inside. That didn't make much of a difference, because the man would block the doorway, shouting curses, until he was given a beer.

Donovan had just stopped in at Riley's to ask George Kohler about Haitians when Halftrack toddled in. Kohler spotted him in a flash.

"Get outta here, you fuck! You're not drinking in this bar!"

"You can't eighty-six me. I'm a cripple."

"I'm not gonna eighty-six you! I'm gonna pour lighter fluid on you and set you on fire, you prick! Get out!"

To make the point perfectly clear, Kohler yanked open the drawer where he kept the dictionary, *Guinness Book of World Records*, *TV Guides*, and other argument-settlers. He pulled out a tin of lighter fluid and pointed it menacingly.

"I demand police protection," Halftrack shot back, moving up alongside Donovan.

Kohler was unfazed. "I mean it. Get the fuck outta here! Do I have to come around the bar and shove you over a cliff?"

"Let him stay," Donovan said. "For one beer anyway."

"No beer! He can have a shot, but no beer! If he has a beer, then he'll have to piss and it takes him twenty minutes. The son of a bitch will tie up the john and we got a lot of pissers in this joint."

"Fleischmann's," Halftrack said.

Kohler left the can of lighter fluid in plain sight on the backbar. "Remember, I got this here in case I need it," he said, and stomped off to get Halftrack a shot.

"That's decent of you, officer," Halftrack said.

"My name's Bill. You know that."

"Sure, sure. What can I do for you? I'm always happy to help out when I get asked nice. Now, this fuck behind the bar . . ."

"Don't start," Donovan snapped. "Just don't start. At least not until you tell me what I want to know."

"What's that?"

"You know every creep on the street."

"Startin' with him," Halftrack said, pointing at Kohler.

"I *warned* you. I'm not gonna pay for your drink if you start getting on peoples' cases again. I'm looking for this Haitian guy who comes in here sometimes. He's about my height, very black, has a little mustache. He drinks Bacardi and tonic."

"You know what he does for a living?"

Donovan shook his head. "I have no idea. He may be a dope dealer, but that's only conjecture."

"Huh?"

"I'm only guessing," Donovan explained.

Halftrack downed his shot, then smiled. "A lot of those guys are orderlies. They work at the hospital. Does this guy come in around seven or eight at night?"

Donovan nodded.

"That could be it, then. One of Roosevelt Hospital's shifts ends at seven. This guy you want . . . does he wear white pants?"

"Not the time I saw him."

"He could still work at Roosevelt. Try that, officer. If it gets you anyplace, you owe me."

"We'll discuss it at the time. If you hear anything about him, my office is above the pawn shop."

"I'm not too good with stairs."

"Throw a rock at the window. I've got to go now."

Halftrack raised his hand and said, "Wait."

"What do you want?" Donovan asked suspiciously.

"You have to help me empty my bag."

Donovan knew that one. Halftrack pissed through a plastic tube which ran from his bladder, through the side of his abdomen, to a plastic bag hung from one of the struts of his walker. He didn't really need help emptying his bag, but few of his victims realized that. He liked to humiliate people who felt required to empty a plastic bag full of urine for a guy who could make perhaps three blocks an hour in his walker. Halftrack (when bartenders would let him) drank copious amounts of beer, assuring himself of frequent bagfuls and many victims. "He's not disliked for no reason," Donovan once observed.

"Empty your own fucking bag," Donovan snapped.

"I can't. If I try to get into the men's room he's gonna dump lighter fluid on me and set me on fire."

"Then empty your bag in the gutter. It's not indecent exposure if all you whip out is a plastic bag."

Camelia Rodriguez beat the hell out of a tennis ball for nearly forty minutes, until the sun was below the New Jersey side of the Hudson and the floodlights had gone on over the handball courts. Her anger over having been stood up was gone, and Camelia had begun to miss Johnny. She wondered what had become of him. If he had to miss their appointment, there must have been a good reason.

Rather than heading straight home, she decided to drop in on him. Silver Shoes lived in a loose communal arrangement with five other American Indians in an old brownstone. Columbia students all, they were experimenting with traditional Indian living arrangements to see how they worked in the Big Apple. Camelia knew nothing of American Indians, only that they made much of her native Cuban Indian blood and treated her like a princess.

When she climbed to the top of the circular stone staircase leading up from the handball courts, she found Riverside Park darker than usual. The infrequently spaced street lamps, working the night before, were out. The poles were only ten feet high. It wasn't hard to do, and the roving bands of vandals who decorated the granite walls with graffiti periodically smashed the lamps. But this time the destruction was systematic; the park was black. No one else seemed to be in the park, either. News of the recent murders had seen to that. It was only Camelia's need to take out her anger on the handball court that kept her in the park too long. As she started across the blackened grass, Camelia finally was afraid.

To the north, the lamps of the tennis courts attracted her. She turned onto one of the asphalt bike paths and made her way in that direction. There would be someone there who could walk her out of the park and up to the relative safety of Riverside Drive. At Eighty-ninth Street, the steepest slope and highest hill in the park rose from river level up to the Soldiers and Sailors Monument. That monolith, constructed at the turn of the century to honor veterans of the Civil War, lorded over a secluded section of woods, weeds, and wild chives visited by few. There was a saxophone player who climbed up there every morning to practice, and a bagpiper who made less frequent visits. At night, the woods around the Soldiers and Sailors Monument were empty. Camelia hated even walking by the spot.

She broke into a jog as her fear at last overcame her. Camelia thought she saw someone on the courts. It was too dark to play at night, even with the lights, but now and then one of the regulars did stay on to practice his serve. Camelia heard a noise; a twig snapped, and a gigantic figure, dressed all in black, broke out of the bushes and lunged at her.

Camelia gasped and swung her racket. It was caught before the blow could land. She screamed, but the scream was cut off as a mammoth paw covered her mouth. She was lifted off the ground by arms that made it seem effortless and, as unconsciousness swept over her, was carried up the hill.

CIRCLE OF FIRE

After leaving Riley's, Donovan spent an hour in his office, reading the day's reports. Jefferson was getting together the complete list of all the stuff in Geffrard's apartment, and the young man's father, in from Port-au-Prince to claim the body, wanted to see Donovan. Two other detectives were completing a list of the residents of the block where the Haitian Donovan was chasing had disappeared. And a Haitian cop was tracked down at a precinct in Queens. He was said to be willing to talk about Haitian voodoo. Donovan initialed the reports and went home.

The apartment smelled of beef and spices. Rosie was in the kitchen, stirring a large pot of chili which steamed deliciously in the cool breeze blowing in off the Hudson. Donovan felt like a married man for the first time in his life and, surprisingly, liked the feeling. He wrapped his arms around her and kissed her on the back of the neck.

"How was your day?" she asked.

"Not good, not bad. These things always take time. What did you do?"

"I cleaned up," she said proudly. "I got all the way through the bedroom. You have a real talent for making a mess, William."

"Talent has nothing to do with it. Hard work is the key. And I *like* the way I live. If the bedroom smells like Lysol, I'm gonna get a big cigar and stink it up."

He got himself a beer, opened it, and wandered into the bedroom. To his surprise, he liked the way the place looked. The linens were washed and pressed, the floor vacuumed and polished, and even the windows were washed. Donovan went to the west window and looked out.

There were no ships on the Hudson, but in the park

below, a circle of fire burned evilly outlining the Soldiers and Sailors Monument. Donovan stared at the fire, horrified and transfixed, for several seconds, then scooped up his walkie-talkie and ran out of the apartment.

The elevator seemed to take forever. Donovan cursed it all the way up and all the way back down to the lobby, but running fifteen flights would have taken longer. He ran through the lobby, bowling over a man carrying groceries, and spun the revolving door furiously as he forced his way through it.

Donovan ran straight across Riverside Drive, ducking the traffic which squealed to a halt in both directions. He drew his gun as he reached the bottom of the stairs leading down into the park. The park seemed empty and, with the street-lights out, the circle of fire atop the hill glowed like a gigantic halo. It was perhaps thirty feet across, a slowly expanding circle of burning leaves and twigs.

A five-foot iron fence separated the wooded hill from an asphalt footpath that curved down to the base of the hill. Donovan jogged down to the base of the hill, rounded the fence, and was at once assaulted by the same terror Camelia had felt. A chill ran down his spine, and he felt the skin on his face tighten. He switched the walkie-talkie from the Crime Unit channel to that servicing Division Five, which reached all patrol cars in northern Manhattan. There were bound to be a few Division Five cars nearby. Donovan brought the radio to his lips and said, almost in a whisper:

"Eight-eight street in Riverside Park. Lieutenant Dono-van needs a backup."

Within seconds he heard the wail of sirens in the distance.

Donovan stuck the radio back on his belt clip and, holding the revolver in front of him, started up the hill toward the ring of fire.

The path was dark and deeply rutted from the rush of spring rains. Naked tree roots were about to trip him at every step. Apart from the sirens and the crackling of the fire, not a sound could be heard.

He heard movement in the bushes to his left. Donovan spun toward it, but too late. A massive fist crashed into the side of his face. The gun discharged as he fell. Someone jumped on him, and as Donovan rolled to get away, the gun slipped from his fingers.

Donovan was standing again, but so was the killer. Donovan feigned with a left, then pounded a tremendous right into the man's gut. The shape grunted, but barely moved, and Donovan went down again as another punch landed. Donovan's fingers reached for his gun, but a gigantic foot came down on his wrist and he heard a guttural laugh. Donovan groped at the foot with his free hand, and for a second his fingers touched something soft. Then the man's other foot landed on the side of his skull and consciousness slipped away.

He was out less than a minute. The sirens were deafening, as headlamps and voices descended on Riverside Park. Police cars poured down through the 96th Street entrance, which had a ramp to accommodate official vehicles. Donovan was looking in vain for his gun when the first car screeched to a halt and blue uniforms helped him to his feet.

"Lieutenant . . . you okay?"

"He's here. Can't have gone far. The son of a bitch has my gun."

Donovan leaned against a tree while his head cleared. He listened to the sound of the park exits being closed off and a search party of monumental size being improvised. It seemed like every cop north of Times Square had poured into Riverside Park.

A uniformed sergeant came over and appointed himself Donovan's protector.

"You're bleeding, lieutenant. Are you sure you're okay?"

"Yeah. Get me some gauze to mop this up with, will you? I also want an evidence team, and this whole area roped off. Nobody goes up this hill but me. I want a footprint search right here where I fought the prick. And find Sergeant Jefferson and tell him to haul his black ass down here."

"Sure thing," the sergeant replied.

"Gimme a shotgun," Donovan said, and was rewarded with a box of gauze tape and a loaded, 12-gauge Remington pump-action shotgun. As the lights of half-a-dozen police cars were trained on the hill, Donovan started up on his own, pressing a wad of sterile bandage against the side of his head.

The circle of fire was largely burned out. It had been set in the thin layer of dry leaves covering the ground of the only clearing atop the hill, and there were only so many leaves. Donovan stepped into it.

He couldn't recognize the body at first, and then he didn't want to. She was laid out like the others, spread-eagled, but with her wrists and ankles tied to metal stakes driven into the ground, not saplings. The palms fronds had not been burned. Outlining the body were several dozen votive candles, and a crown of corn kernels lay under Camelia's head. From just under the left side of her rib cage, a single dagger lay still implanted in her heart. Donovan fell to his knees, his face contorted. He bent over, like a man shot in the stomach, until his forehead nearly touched the dead girl's foot. Then he straightened, stood, and wiped his eyes with the same blood-soaked bandage he had used for the wounds on his face.

When he got back down to the bottom of the hill, Jefferson had showed up, out of breath and looking uncharacteris-

tically bedraggled. He looked at Donovan and said, "Christ
. . . what the fuck happened?"

"Did you find him?" Donovan asked the uniformed sergeant.

"Nothing so far. I don't know where the hell he went,
lieutenant. We got all the exits covered, and cars watching
the West Side Highway. Don't worry . . . we'll cover every
inch."

Donovan returned the shotgun, and turned to Jefferson.
"The dead girl is Rosie's sister. Cover her up for me, would
you? Close the park. Nobody in, nobody out. Get the evidence team to make a cast of every goddam footprint on this
hill. Everything that even *looks* like a footprint. I'll be back
in two hours. I want the medical examiner's office here *in
force.*"

"I'm sorry, Bill. Jesus, I am."

Donovan started out of the park, nodding vaguely in
response to Jefferson's profession of sympathy.

By the time he climbed the steps at Eighty-ninth Street,
Donovan had a clean piece of gauze against the wounds on
his head. Still, his clothes were dirty and bloodied, and his
face coated with dirt, blood, and tears. A large crowd had
gathered on the terrace surrounding the Soldiers and Sailors
Monument, and uniformed officers were putting wooden
barricades in place. Police radios rang with messages. By the
time he got through the barricade, two shotgun-wielding
cops had joined him as unasked-for bodyguards. The crowd
parted for him, and as he crossed the mall, Donovan saw
Rosie standing at his building beside one of the doormen.

She ran to him and hugged him.

"Come with me," he said, placing her under his arm.

"You're hurt! William . . . what happened? Let me look
at where you're hurt!"

"Come with me," he said, more firmly that time, and led her to his apartment.

THE INFANTA

Donovan stood by the window of the Rodriguez apartment, looking out on Amsterdam Avenue. The neon lights over the hero shop flashed on and off, filling the room with sick yellow light. Off in the background, women were weeping. Donovan stood, staring out the window in silence, a grotesque patch of dried blood still clinging to the side of his face. Santos Rodriguez came over to him. The father had cried enough, and now his face was set with determination.

"She was my baby. My infanta."

Donovan said nothing.

"You find the man who did this. I kill him."

Donovan turned to Rodriguez.

"No. If you kill him, you'll go to jail. You can help me find him. Then . . . *I'll* kill him."

Rodriguez looked at Donovan with wild eyes.

"I owe it to you," Donovan said.

NOTHING

The exhaustive search of Riverside Park yielded no suspects.

"I don't know where the fuck he went, lieutenant," was an oft-heard refrain.

"You ought to have that taken care of," Jefferson said, indicating the damage to Donovan's face.

"In time. I want the medical examiner to look at me first."

"What for? You're not dead. You just *look* like you are."

"Can the jollity, Pancho. I got my reasons. I want a complete run-down on foreign objects in that wound on my face."

"Don't you know what hit you?"

"I got a rough idea it was a fist and a foot."

"So?"

"So there was something wrong with the foot. I felt it, when it stomped on my wrist. The guy had his foot wrapped in something."

"Like what?"

"I don't know. Something soft. I want to find out if there's any of it in my face."

"This guy wore gloves on his feet?" Jefferson asked.

"Maybe," Donovan replied.

Jefferson shook his head, but made the requisite notes. After a moment, he spoke up. "I'm not sayin' I know what this is all about, but the footprint guys say they've never seen anything like the prints they've been getting in this mud."

"Oh?"

"Big and soft, like the guy wore snowshoes. I don't know. What can you wear on your feet that's big and soft?"

"Gloves," Donovan replied.

"We'd better go down to the medical examiner's office. He doesn't have the stuff here to do the job on your head. And I think there's something seriously wrong with it, lieutenant."

DIRT, BLOOD, TWIGS, LEAVES, AND COTTON

"It looks like a bargain sale in there," he said.

The medical examiner had a sense of humor. In his business, as in Donovan's, it was necessary.

"What did you find?" Donovan asked, staring with faint interest at the array of sparkling medical instruments in the Mex's downtown office.

"Aside from skin tissue and beard, there's dirt, blood, twigs, leaves, and cotton. You want to know what kind of tree the leaves came from?"

"No. I want to know what kind of cloth the cotton came from."

"Two kinds. From the gauze, which you were thoughtful enough to bring with you."

"Thoughtfulness had nothing to do with it. Without the gauze, I'd be soaked in blood up to the elbows. That guy packed one fuck of a wallop."

"The rest looks like it's from a white t-shirt. The size of thread and type of weave on the fragment I pulled out of your chin look typical of a cheap t-shirt. You want me to patch you up?"

"Sure," Donovan said, and lapsed into silence as the doctor cleaned and bandaged the several wounds on his face.

"You have two types of damage, lieutenant," the medical examiner went on. "You have a bruise typical of being hit by a man's fist. And you have a broader wound which includes some ripping and tearing. That one gave you the blood. It's also the one I got the cotton out of. The cotton was deeply embedded. The dirt, twigs, and other stuff were closer to the surface. You must have rolled in them after you got hit."

"He's lucky that's all he rolled in," Jefferson chimed in.

"What's the second wound typical of?" Donovan asked.

"Being kicked by a shoe wrapped in cotton cloth, like you thought," the medical examiner said. "Though it beats me why anyone would do that—in New York, anyway. There's some precedent for wrapping shoes in cloth in the Arctic, I think. Eskimos . . . you know."

Donovan said that he understood. When his face was bandaged, he climbed down from the examining table normally reserved for cadavers and walked slowly to where Camelia Rodriguez was laid out. Rigor had set in, and she looked stiff, ashen, unreal, like a plastic statue of the Madonna from Woolworth's. The medical examiner swept a plastic evidence bag off the table and handed it to Donovan.

"The murder weapon," he said.

Donovan turned the instrument over and over in his hand. It was a very old knife, much worn, with a plain blade and a wooden handle. The handle was carved with tiny figures which were almost worn off by age and frequent use —a horse, a godlike figure with the horns of a buffalo, an eagle, and several shapes Donovan couldn't make out. One of these resembled a cross in a square. Donovan gave the knife to Jefferson, who put it in his briefcase.

"This one has the same bruises and wounds as the other two, lieutenant," the doctor said. "Since the palm fronds were left on, there's little doubt they also caused the wrist bruises on the first two. There's the same slice on the left wrist as on the first two . . ."

"Was a quart of blood taken?"

"I'll tell you tomorrow, but it looks that way."

"Any saliva on the wound?"

"Nope. None on the first two, either. If your man drank the blood, he didn't do it straight from the wound."

"What's he do? Put it in a thermos and take it home with him?"

The medical examiner shrugged. Donovan and Jefferson headed for the door, but were stopped. "This one struggled more than the others," the medical examiner said.

"The others expected to be raped," Donovan nodded. "Camelia knew better."

A RAY OF SUNSHINE ENTERS THE CASE

Jefferson occasionally found himself in a mood for summing up. He liked to use the big blackboard in the unit office to chalk lists where everyone could see them. He sent memos summing up the day's progress or lack of it. He was very orderly. For Donovan, who wasn't orderly at all, this came as a blessing.

Jefferson got into one of his summing up moods while riding the elevator up to Donovan's apartment. "The way I see it, lieutenant, we got two possible angles to this case —a Haitian angle and a Cuban angle."

"All three victims were Cuban."

"Yeah, and there's a third angle, if you consider that all three girls went to the same school."

"I don't consider it," Donovan said. "All public school kids that age in this neighborhood go to P.S. 487."

"Just the same, it may be important to keep in mind."

"You keep it in mind. I have other things to think about."

"Such as?"

"Does that knife remind you of anything?"

"Not particularly," Jefferson admitted.

"Don't you remember? Last week Art Theft sent around a flyer describing stuff stolen from the Museum of the American Indian. You know . . . the joint on upper Broadway."

"Yeah, now that you mention it."

"I think the murder weapon is one of the stolen items," Donovan said.

"That's easy enough to check out," Jefferson said, a ray of sunshine entering the case at last.

"Do it tonight. One more thing . . . what did you say were Camelia's movements before she was killed?"

"From what I gather, she left your apartment and went to the tennis courts. She hung around a while, talked to the attendant . . ."

"Who?"

"Your friend, Rolland Gomez."

"And when her partner didn't show up, she left. That's all I could learn."

"Who was her partner?" Donovan asked. "Her boyfriend?"

"That's what Gomez says."

Donovan sighed, looked down and shook his head. The action hurt his jaw, at a spot where the bandage ran down the jawline nearly to his neck.

"Come on into the apartment," he said.

"Hey, you're gonna want to be alone with your girl. This ain't the time for a social call."

"It ain't social," Donovan said. "Geffrard told me something that night I talked to him. He said, by way of defending Haitian customs, that only two groups in this hemisphere practiced human sacrifice—Aztecs and Pawnees."

Donovan unlocked the door to his apartment and led his sergeant inside. Rosie jumped up to meet them. Her face was haggard from crying, her hands locked in front of her.

"What kind of Indian is Johnny Silver Shoes?" he asked.

"What do you mean?" She was confused.

"What tribe?"

"Pawnee, I'm pretty sure," she replied.

Donovan turned to Jefferson. "Find him for me." Without a word, Jefferson hurried out the door.

"You can't think that Johnny killed my sister," Rosie said, aghast at this new shock. "What about the Haitians?"

"On the back burner for a while."

"But . . . *Johnny?*"

"He's a Pawnee experimenting in upholding tribal traditions even in New York. One Pawnee tradition is human sacrifice. And Camelia was killed with a ceremonial Pawnee knife stolen from a museum. Furthermore, Johnny knew that she would be in the park and when. He was supposed to meet her and didn't. Or maybe he *did* meet her, and killed her. At any rate, I think he has to explain himself."

Rosie nodded, and let herself be gathered up in Donovan's arms. They hugged for a long time, not speaking until he asked how her parents were bearing up.

"Dad's okay. Mom is still inconsolable, though. I have to go back. I just wanted to see how you are and . . . I forgot to shut off the oven."

Donovan patted her on the head. "Never mind. I'll get you a cab."

She stepped back, brushed a strand of hair from her cheek, and touched his bandaged jaw. "Are you all right? You look awful."

"I feel awful, but the bleeding has stopped, and I got some useful information from my scars. You don't happen to know what sort of footgear Pawnees wear, do you?"

"Johnny always wears tennis shoes. Look, William, I have to go."

She started off, but he held her arm. "I'm sorry about Camelia. It was my fault, I know. I should have had the park shut down at night after the second murder."

Rosie pulled away. "I don't want to talk about it," she said, going to the door and yanking it open.

"Can I see you tomorrow?" Donovan asked.

"No. I need time."

Donovan nodded.

"You made a promise to my father," she went on. "I expect you to keep it, even if Johnny is the one."

BLACK IRISH

Johnny Silver Shoes and his other Indian friends had turned their old brownstone—once a fraternity house and, for a while, a "free university" offering courses in organic cooking, solar energy, and the like—into a haven of Pawnee Indian lore. It was, actually, a center of rather homogenous Indian lore, for the number of available posters, books, and paintings on the Pawnees was limited indeed.

The four floors of the dirty, old building were hung with color posters of redmen in canoes, redmen on horses, and desert vistas and forest scenes which might have been snipped from *National Geographic.* Dog-eared copies of the paperbound edition of *Bury My Heart at Wounded Knee* were conspicuous on coffee tables (made from orange crates and planks), and there was even one framed eight by ten of a vastly overweight Marlon Brando nearly breaking a horse's back in *The Missouri Breaks.* Donovan was slightly disappointed. The Pawnee chauvinism of Johnny Silver Shoes' little commune was not as rigorous as he had imagined.

When Donovan got there, Jefferson had been impressing the group with the power of the police for several hours. Jefferson had, through the sheer force of his personality, developed a talent for terrorizing suspects that had been the province of Irish sergeants for generations. His patter was different, but the effect was the same. Donovan walked in just as Jefferson was finishing a description of life in Attica State Prison. The description left nothing to the imagination. Jefferson was beyond doubt an up-and-comer, and Donovan was duly proud of his protégé.

Donovan went with Johnny Silver Shoes up to his rooms and sat him down on the old, cotton-covered couch salvaged from the garbage of a Columbia apartment building down the block.

Silver Shoes was sweating and nervous. After he sat down, Donovan grumbled, "Stand up."

Johnny did as he was told. Donovan walked over to him, grasped the hem of his white tennis shirt, and pulled it up to look at the Indian's stomach. It looked tan, not red, but convention was convention.

"Do you bruise easily?" Donovan asked.

"I . . . I don't think so," Johnny replied.

"Let's find out." Donovan took Johnny's left arm, and

delivered a sharp blow halfway up from the elbow. Johnny winced and yanked his arm away.

"Hey, what the hell's this?" he asked.

"An innocence test, Johnny. I gave the guy who killed Camelia one fuck of a right to the gut. He'd have a bruise, if he bruises like most people do. I got a good right hand. I don't land it often, but when I do, I do damage. Your gut is pristine. I just gave your arm a tap to see how your body responds to damage."

"I understand," Johnny said, backing away.

"Sit down," Donovan said, and to Jefferson added, "I want the same test performed on the other five guys in this house. If any of them bitch about it, tell them you're a draft board and this is a short-arm examination. If none of 'em know what the fuck that is, I leave it up to your discretion."

"Sure thing, lieutenant," Jefferson said, and was off.

When the two of them were alone, Johnny Silver Shoes lowered his head and shook it. "I don't know how you could think I killed her," he said.

"Why didn't you show up for your appointment to play tennis with her?" Donovan asked.

"I forgot I was supposed to play tennis that day. I'm a busy man, lieutenant. Getting through Columbia isn't as easy as making bruises on people."

"I know cops who make better bruises than me. My father was one. What were you doing at the hour Camelia expected you on the courts?"

"I was here, getting stinkin' drunk."

"Why?"

"Why not? I have my problems. My friends and I were drinkin' and bullshittin'. That's the way it was."

"And you forgot about Camelia?" Donovan asked.

"It's happened before. Ask her folks."

Donovan reached inside his jacket and took out the murder weapon, still in its plastic bag.

"Ever see this before?"

Silver Shoes looked at the knife with a mixture of fascination and horror.

"That . . . my God!"

"Yeah," Donovan said. "This is a Pawnee ceremonial dagger, stolen from the Museum of the American Indian. Sergeant Jefferson had the curator identify it just this evening. Camelia was killed with it."

"I've seen that knife. I spend a lot of time at the Museum. I . . . I didn't know it was stolen." He buried his head in his hands, then looked back at Donovan. "I see why you think I killed her."

"Damned decent of you. Most people aren't so understanding when they're accused of murder."

"*Are* you accusing me?"

Donovan chose not to answer the question, but instead asked for a description of Pawnee human sacrifice. Silver Shoes stuttered a moment, then tossed his hands up in despair. "It's not really my specialty. We don't exactly play it up as having been a part of our history. All I know is that a young girl was painted, killed, and I think her body was cut up and distributed around the corn fields."

"A spring ritual?"

"Look, lieutenant, my professor knows a lot more about it than me. Why don't you ask him? I'll write down his name and number."

As he did so, Jefferson came back up the stairs. "Everyone's clean, boss. If you nailed one of 'em in the gut, he doesn't show it."

Donovan nodded reluctantly. Silver Shoes had not bruised where Donovan hit him on the arm. And none of the six Indians seemed big enough to have been the massive figure Donovan had fought in the park. Still, if a man wore special footgear and perhaps other padding . . . .

Silver Shoes handed Donovan a slip of paper which he folded and put in his pocket.

"How many people know about this living arrangement you have here?"

"Lots. We're proud of the commune. There have even been articles in the paper about us, and we were interviewed for "Good Morning, America" once. Why do you ask?"

"For one thing, I never heard of this place before I had dinner with you that Sunday afternoon at the Rodriguez apartment. For another thing, if you didn't murder Camelia Rodriguez, somebody sure is going to a lot of trouble to make it look that way."

Dawn was breaking over Riverside Park. Donovan and Jefferson had been up all night, and had a busy day ahead of them. The hill was roped off, and uniformed cops still guarded the approaches. Evidence teams were doing a leaf-by-leaf search of the whole area. So far, nothing had been found but the usual garbage—beer bottles, used condoms, Burger King wrappers, and rumpled copies of the *Post* and the *Racing Form*.

"Can you believe a group of guys stabbin' chicks to death as a kind of rite of spring?" Jefferson said. "I mean, I seen some weird shit in my time, but that takes the cake."

"And then leaving a message . . ."

"The knife," Jefferson cut in.

". . . to let us know this was an Indian thing, as if the thought hadn't already occurred to us," Donovan said. "Whoever did this wants to make sure everyone knows it's a ritual, and not only a ritual, but a Pawnee one."

"You think it's Silver Ass, or whatever his name is?"

"I don't know. He *is* in the business of taking pride in his heritage. We only have his word that he's not proud of the human sacrifice part of that heritage. Anyone who's that caught up in his peoples' history to pull off human sacrifice ain't gonna have too many qualms about leaving the knife behind to let us know about it. On the other hand, if the killer *isn't* Silver Shoes and his lot, we have another problem."

"What's that?"

"Why is someone trying to blame it on him?"

"It's easy," Jefferson said.

"Yeah, it's easy. He's a perfect target. But that means the killer has to know about the Indian commune as well as the fact that Pawnees practiced human sacrifice and that a ceremonial dagger was in the museum. That's a nice bit of research. Of course, with anyone who's into human sacrifice I imagine we can presume dedication."

"So what you're saying is that the Indians did it, the Haitians did it, or X did it."

"That's what I'm saying," Donovan replied.

NO PRINTS

There were no fingerprints on the knife, which had been wiped clean. That fit in with any of a dozen explanations for the murders, and Donovan didn't give it much thought.

The plaster casts of the footprints made by the man Donovan fought were fourteen inches long and nearly half as wide.

"*That's* what you can tell the press," Jefferson said gleefully. "The killer is Sasquatch."

"Who?"

"Bigfoot. Don't you watch TV, lieutenant?"

"Only war movies and football games."

"Yeah, well I don't think even Mean Joe Green has feet that big."

"The whole thing doesn't sound very Pawnee to me," Donovan said. "On the other hand, these rituals are kind of a mixed bag anyway. I doubt there were too many votive candles in the Nebraska territory a few hundred years ago. I have to talk to that Columbia professor whose name Silver Shoes wrote down for me. Where the hell did I put it?"

He fumbled through the jumble of change, pencil stubs, and crumpled memoranda in his pockets.

"Before you talk to him, you got to talk to the commissioner, the press, and that Haitian cat who's come up for Geffrard's body."

"And every one of them wants to fry my ass," Donovan said, taking the paper Silver Shoes had given him from his pocket and unfolding it.

Donovan squinted at the name, then rubbed his eyes.

"What the hell's wrong?" Jefferson asked.

"Silver Shoes' professor? He's my friend Jack."

DONOVAN BECOMES A CELEBRITY

One reporter implied that Donovan should have beaten the shit out of the man in the park the night before, not the other way around.

"Muhammad Ali couldn't have done better," Donovan maintained, to which the reporter replied, "Muhammad Ali is retired."

To his credit, Donovan did look like shit. His original bandage was still on, covering a goodly portion of the left side of his face. The department's plan for dealing with the press during protracted crises called for Donovan to phony up looking bedraggled. It was not necessary to phony up Donovan's appearance this time.

"Look," Donovan said, his patience worn thin, "I took on a hidden assailant in a park that was totally dark. The man is a known murderer, certainly insane, and he jumped me from behind a bush. I'm lucky I got through it as well as I did."

As it turned out, the point was well taken. Donovan came off being portrayed as a cop who had risked his life trying to catch a murderer. The press began to shift their attention from the facts of the case to the force of Donovan's personality. This was just as well. Though they weren't told key facts such as the origin of the dagger, and no one said the words "Indian" or "Haitian" in public when referring to the case, one enterprising journalist got hold of the information that Camelia Rodriguez was the sister of Donovan's girlfriend. This increased the number of stories centering around Donovan. In the tabloids, his case had become a holy quest, an impassioned search for vengeance. That is, in fact, what it was.

NO MORE DEFENSIVE WAR

Riverside Park was closed at dusk. Cops were positioned at every entrance between Seventy-second and Ninety-sixth streets to enforce the edict.

The move was largely cosmetic. Not many people were going into the park at night anyway. The mall was busy with joggers and dog walkers, but few persons wanted to brave the darkness beneath that big, cold wall.

"I'm tired of fighting a defensive war," Donovan said. "I'm going out looking for that son of a bitch."

Jefferson offered a quizzical look.

"Where's Marcie working these days?" Donovan asked.

"Oh, no. Come on, man, you don't wanna start that up again."

"I need her."

"She's at Midtown South, but . . . I mean it, man . . ."

"I'm not gonna *marry* the girl," Donovan said. "I just need her help."

"You know what happens when the two of you get together. What about Rosie?"

"She's not talking to me, but that's beside the point. Marcie is the best we got for what I have in mind."

"What are you gonna do? Dress her up in tennis duds and march her back and forth through the park?"

"Something like that," Donovan said.

"Oh, *shit*. You're a glutton for punishment, you know it?"

"The possibility has occurred to me," Donovan said.

SATAN IS THE ENEMY

Alexander Geffrard was a small, thin man, with rimless spectacles and a tiny mustache that barely extended to the corners of his lips. He was very black, and conservatively dressed in a fine tweed suit that appeared to have been custom made. He looked more like a stockbroker than the petty official in the Haitian government he was said to be, and seemed very out of place in the grubby office of the West Side Major Crimes Unit.

"It is good of you to see me, lieutenant," he said, shaking Donovan's hand and taking the metal chair in front of Donovan's desk.

"No problem. I'm sorry about your son, Mr. Geffrard."

"That's *Captain* Geffrard."

"Oh. Is that Army or Navy?"

"Neither. I am a policeman, a colleague of yours."

"That would be the Tontons Macoute, then?" Donovan asked, unwilling to consider a member of Haiti's notorious secret police a colleague.

"You know of my department?"

"Only by reputation. Like I said, Captain, I'm very sorry about your son. I promise you, I will do my best to see that justice is done."

Geffrard smiled faintly, and nodded. "May I ask if you have a suspect?"

"Yes, but I don't know his name." Donovan told about meeting Peter Geffrard at Riley's, their conversation, and the events that followed.

"Why were you asking my son about voodoo? Is it in connection with your other case?"

"*Other* case? Yes, it was. I was using your son as an expert witness of sorts. I asked him about voodoo, and he explained that human sacrifice is not a part of it."

"I assure you that it is not," Geffrard said quickly. "My son would not be a part of anything illegal."

"Then why was he killed, captain? I hate to be so blunt about it, but his murder was in the manner of an execution, and his apartment was searched."

Donovan expected Geffrard to be angry. He was disappointed. The Haitian showed no emotion at all. "My son was studying to be a man of the cloth. He would not have been involved in voodoo, nor would he have known anyone with that inclination. True, there are some in my country who drink too much and pull the heads off chickens, but Peter would not have known them."

"He knew *something* that his murderer thought he was

imparting to me," Donovan said. "If not voodoo, what? Did he have enemies?"

"Everyone has enemies."

"Even men of the cloth?"

"Especially men of the cloth, for whom Satan is the enemy."

Donovan shook his head sadly. This was getting nowhere.

"All right, Captain Geffrard," he said, "leave me your cable address and I'll keep you informed."

When the man was gone, Donovan called for Jefferson. "Make an appointment for me tomorrow with Bill Keane of West Side Narcotics."

Jefferson nodded and made a note on his pad.

"Who do we know at Immigration?"

"Unh . . . I don't know. Wait, John Flaherty is our man over there. You want to see him tomorrow, too?"

"Yeah. I'm going over to Jack's apartment now. I'm going alone. I wouldn't inflict him on anyone else."

KLIBAN CATS AND CUISINARTS

Jack's apartment looked different. Once it had been pleasantly middle-class academic, with floor-to-ceiling bookshelves, tote bags bearing the logotype of the local public television station, and cardboard boxes holding ten years' back issues of *The New Yorker*. Kliban cats had perched on couches and shelves, and a Cuisinart had flanked dozens of matching Bell jars holding spices, beans, rice, and pasta.

Then Lois moved out of Jack's apartment and into that of her lover, the mysterious fellow whose name Donovan wished he had the time to figure out. Donovan was eager to burst the balloon of her mystery, and imagined himself knocking on the door of her love hideout one evening with a bottle of ordinary red wine and a silly grin. Unfortunately, he hadn't the time. Dealing with Jack was quite enough, especially when the interview was conducted in an apartment which Donovan recalled as being rich and full of life. Now the four rooms on Riverside Drive were barren: the bookshelves had wide gaps, as if teeth had been pulled out; the toy stuffed cats were gone, and the Cuisinart was just a memory, a spot on the counter free of dust and cooking oil. Cockroaches prowled the dog dish, the dog having fled with the woman who paid for its food.

Donovan felt uncomfortable. It was the first time he had been in the place since Jack and Lois split up. He was not uncomfortable enough to feel less angry. Jack was holding out on him, and maybe worse.

"What the fuck is going on?" Donovan asked. "You never told me you were teaching. You said you were getting your doctorate."

"I am," Jack replied, obviously put off his feet. "But I also teach one undergraduate course a year. A lot of people do it when they get close to their doctorates."

"What course are you teaching?"

" 'Tribal Art in the Twentieth Century.' "

"Including the art of the Indians on the Bay of Campeche?" Donovan asked.

"Including them. Why do you ask? What's this all about, Bill?"

"Those Mexican Indians . . . they're Aztecs, aren't they?"

"Yes, they are the direct descendents of the Aztecs."

"Do you also study their tradition of human sacrifice?"

"So that's what it's all about," Jack said with a sigh.

"That's it. And it's about Johnny Silver Shoes, one of your students."

"The Pawnee Indian. So? Wait . . . I know what you're getting at . . . they also have a tradition of human sacrifice."

"Bingo," Donovan said.

"Do you think that Johnny Silver Shoes and I are running around Riverside Park conducting blood sacrifices?"

"Is that what you're doing?"

Jack whistled softly between his teeth. "Wow . . . it's come to this for you and me, has it?"

"Our relationship has nothing to do with it. No, it *has* something to do with it. As your friend, I haven't been able to help noticing you've been a mite unstable recently."

"Now, wait a minute."

"Jesus, you were into Cuban checkout clerks a month ago. What the fuck is it now? High school girls?"

"Sonia told you that, didn't she?"

"She did."

"I . . . Jesus Christ!" He couldn't get out what he meant to say, and lapsed into silence. Donovan wouldn't let him off the hook.

"You jumped into the fast lane both feet first. I don't care about that, so long as it doesn't border on anything illegal. Screwing high-school girls is illegal, but marginally so as long as they agree. What I want to know is, are you into hurting them at the same time?"

"I don't believe in hurting anyone."

"What about Johnny Silver Shoes?"

"He's a good student with a fine future. He's studying tribal societies and technological change in preparation for a career leading his people."

"Politics."

"Yes. Johnny wants to run for Congress in his home

district in a few years. Eventually, he'd like to be in the Senate. I can't see him doing anything to jeopardize that future."

"Okay," Donovan said, "tell me about Pawnee rituals."

"The one you're interested in was pretty ghastly. Specifics varied a lot, but the general idea is that a fifteen-year-old girl . . ."

"Fifteen?" Donovan asked.

"Yes. She was selected by the men of the tribe and, for six months, treated royally. She was given gifts by the young men of the tribe, and so on. When the fatal day came, her body was painted . . . in what manner I can't say . . . and she was killed. Then her body was cut up and the parts distributed around the cornfields. It was a spring ritual, like most blood sacrifices."

"Were corn kernels a part of it?"

"Yes. They were usually a part of the ceremony. A handful of kernels kept over the winter was used ceremonially to begin the new growing season. Were they a part of your murders?"

Donovan nodded. "But palms weren't," he said.

"Of course not. The Pawnee lived in Nebraska and Oklahoma. Palms are part of Caribbean rituals."

"Aztec?"

"Yes," Jack said begrudgingly. "But let me tell you one thing. All the stuff I told you is available in popular histories. There's nothing very secretive about Aztec or Pawnee rituals. They're pretty gruesome, but details aren't hard to find."

"Anyone could learn this stuff?" Donovan asked.

"Absolutely anyone."

"Where were you yesterday between the hours of four and eight?"

"Between four and eight? I went to Zabar's, bought some

stuff, then came home. I stopped at the deli on the corner
to buy cigarettes, and aside from that I was home the whole
time."

"Alone?"

"Absolutely alone," Jack said.

TOO MUCH FOR GRASS, TOO LITTLE FOR COCAINE

"You woulda felt right at home living in Geffrard's apartment," Jefferson said. "He had as much crap on the floor as you do. I know because I got it all indexed."

"Anything of interest?"

"Let's start with the address book. You know that Riley's phone number is in there. There are three other bars, too. One of 'em is on Columbus and the other's on Amsterdam."

"Name 'em."

"Patrino's on Columbus and Ninety-ninth. The Orange Blossom on Amsterdam and One hundred and first. Orbison's on Amsterdam and Seventy-eighth. The guy must have drunk as much as you do."

"Guys who drink cognac are seldom serious drinkers. It costs too much for one thing. If Geffrard wrote down the names of a lot of bars, it was for some reason other than thirst."

"He had contacts there," Jefferson went on.

"Yeah, but for what purpose? Did you find anything else?"

"You remember the Miró print on the wall?"

Donovan remembered.

"The first time we went through the joint, we didn't look at the back of the print. Well, taped to the back was a piece of typing paper with a bunch of figures on it. It was typed on Geffrard's typewriter."

"What kind of figures?"

"Initials, dates, and amounts of money," Jefferson said.

"Money as in betting?"

"I don't think so. They were middle figures, all in the four hundred to seven hundred dollar range. Too much for grass, pills, or the ponies, and too little for cocaine. Look at this."

He showed Donovan a Xerox of the sheet in question. Donovan stared at it for a time, then put it aside. "Did Geffrard have a bank account?"

"Two, but nothing out of the ordinary. However, Chemical Bank says he . . ."

"Got a lot of money from home," Donovan cut in.

"Nope. *Sent* a lot of money home. Every month, Geffrard put a bank check for a few thousand bucks in an envelope and mailed it to Haiti."

"Curiouser and curiouser," Donovan replied.

"Ain't it just."

HIGH YELLOW

The West Side Major Crimes Unit came to a screeching halt when Sergeant Marcia Barnes walked in. She was tall and beautiful, a light-skinned black woman with Alpine features, silky black hair that didn't need to be processed, and demeanor of a high order. When Jefferson saw her, he grinned.

"Well, if it ain't High Yellow," he said.

"Jealousy is unbecoming," she replied, and walked past him to embrace Donovan.

"Hello, Marcie."

"Donovan. You called. It's good to see you again."

They kissed, and she helped herself to a chair near his. With a glance, he got his men back about their business.

"How's the hooker business in midtown?" he asked.

"Good, as always. How are *you* doing? I see you on television a lot."

"The price of fame."

"The price looked too steep the other day. You looked beat, if you don't mind my saying so."

"I *was* beat, and I don't mind your saying so. Will you help me?"

"Sure. Haven't I always done what you wanted? Besides, I'm tired of pretending to be a Working Girl. Busting johns is humiliating. But if you think you can get me to look like a teenage Cuban girl . . ."

"I have no such hope." It was a reasonable assessment on Donovan's part. Marcia Barnes looked a classy, sexy twenty-eight, and not at all like someone who'd been walking through the park on her way home from school. But she was a second-degree black belt, and had decent acting instincts.

"The guy I'm after seems to have been working up in age. The last victim was fifteen. I figure the next to be eighteen. You can look eighteen."

"So you're going to plant me in Riverside Park and paint a bullseye on my ass, is that it?"

"Crudely put, but essentially correct," Donovan admitted.

She touched his hand, which had been extended across the desk for just such an eventuality.

"Will you be there too?" she asked.

He nodded.

"I'll do it, then. I *have* missed you, Donovan. I was even jealous when I read about your Cuban girlfriend."

He began to laugh, suppressed it, then averted his eyes.

"No, I *was* jealous. I missed you. You should have married me when you had the chance."

"As I recall," he said, "we both had the chance. I asked you once, and you said no. You asked me once, and I said no. Whose turn is it now? Shall we flip a coin?"

She nodded. "*My* coin, darling. Yours has always been crooked."

A CLASS ACT

"This park has really gone downhill since I was a kid," Marcie observed.

"No kidding," Donovan said. "I can remember when this place was a class act. The toilets worked, and there were even washroom attendants to shine your shoes. You had families walking after church on Sunday. Now every day looks like a goddam garbage scene. At least the guy we're after has reduced attendance somewhat."

They walked arm in arm through the park, as Donovan gave her a tour of the murder scenes. It was late in the day, and they were practically alone. Those who weren't afraid of the police curfew were terrified of the killer.

"Tell me, Donovan, is it one guy we're looking for?"

"Everybody asks me that, and to tell you the truth, I don't know. I have a personal grudge against the one guy who made this little filigree on my face. There could be a group. If it's Aztec, Pawnee, or Haitian, it has to be a group activity.

The business with the feet being wrapped doesn't fit either of those, but what the hell, this *is* lunacy we're dealing with."

Marcie walked Donovan over to that section of walkway where the park overlooked the West Side Highway.

"Don't be too hard on yourself for losing him," she said. "He could have gone onto the highway and been a mile away in no time."

"It isn't just that," Donovan explained. "I take it as a personal affront that he did it all right under my window. Sometimes I think the last one was aimed at me."

"Donovan," she asked, "is there any chance the man who's doing this is a friend of yours?"

"I'm looking into the possibility."

She hoisted herself up on the short concrete wall just above the highway and the river. He joined her, and they looked up at Donovan's apartment building, which poked above the tree level and menaced the park like a hilltop boulder.

"You left your bedroom light on," she said with a smile.

"I know. I did it on purpose."

"Why? So you can find your way home? I realize you're Irish."

"Welcome back into my life, kid," Donovan said with a grin that matched hers. "I did it to find out just how many of these murder sites are directly visible from my apartment."

"Well?"

"All of them."

"It could be important," she said. "On the other hand, you have a dynamite view. I'm going to enjoy having it back."

"I beg your pardon?" Donovan wasn't really surprised.

"I'll be staying at your place, of course. I live on the East Side now. You don't seriously expect me to take the bus to work every day."

Donovan shook his head.

"I'll take one of the spare rooms if you've suddenly gone moral."

"I haven't."

"It happens to men your age, you know. As for your girlfriend . . ."

"She's not my girlfriend," Donovan said. "The press created that fiction. We went out two or three times and she stayed at my place four, maybe five nights. When a girl gets off work at four in the morning and you get together afterwards, it's kind of unreasonable to expect her to go home alone."

"I understand, Donovan," Marcie said, clearly amused by his uptightness.

"Fuck you," he growled.

"I sincerely hope so."

Marcie jumped off the concrete wall and brushed off her slacks. "Come on, Donovan, you can help me pick out a tennis outfit. I hope the commissioner gave you a big budget, 'cause my taste has gotten a lot more expensive since the last time we went around together."

But he didn't go shopping with her. He went to his office to work. With Marcie around, the temptation to fuck off would be overwhelming anyway. He couldn't give in to it so soon.

THE AMERICAN EMBASSY, PANAMA CITY, 1959

The rock came up from Broadway, hit the window, cracked it, and sent tiny pieces of glass flying into the container of coffee sent up from the donut shop.

Donovan scowled at his coffee, looked up, and said, "It's

like being in Panama that time they were bringing down the flag. What the fuck is goin' on?"

Jefferson surveyed the situation and reported that "a bald guy in an orthopedic walker covered with all kindsa crap threw a rock through the window. You want I should have him arrested, lieutenant?"

Donovan felt his head, which was hurting from the pain of a new headache. "No," he said. "I told him to do it. I'll go down and have a talk with him."

Halftrack was perched by the curb, drinking sweet wine from a pint bottle and looking proud as a pig in shit for having broken the unit's window after having been invited to do so. "You still looking for this guy from Haiti?" he asked when Donovan got downstairs. "You want him? I may know where he is."

"Bacardi and tonic? Little mustache?"

"That's the guy. He drinks at Patrino's, the place on Columbus and Ninety-ninth. Every night around seven or eight he comes in, has a few, and takes a few calls."

"A few calls? Every night?"

"Yeah," Halftrack confirmed. "The barkeep thinks he's a bookie."

"How do *you* get over to Columbus and Ninety-ninth? I make it close to a mile, and you only can do two or three blocks an hour in that contraption."

"A trade secret, lieutenant. That'll be a hundred bucks."

"When I catch the guy you get the bread. Let's not be greedy."

"I'm not greedy. Only thirsty."

"Twenty now, another thirty when I get him," Donovan said.

"Hey!"

"*And* another fifty if the tip leads me to the killer."

Halftrack shrugged and turned his walker south toward Eighty-sixth Street. That was a major crosstown boulevard, and a good corner on which to stand and start fights. Donovan pushed a twenty into his shirt pocket.

By the time Donovan climbed back up the stairs to the unit headquarters, Sergeant Jefferson was just off the phone, where he had been dickering with a glazier.

"I tell you, lieutenant, there ain't no justice anymore. You got any idea how much it's gonna cost to get that window fixed?"

"I don't want to know. How long do you think it would take to get a wiretap put on the pay phone at Patrino's. You know, the joint at Ninety-ninth and Columbus?"

"Five, maybe six hours."

"That's too late for tonight," Donovan said. "Put it in the works anyway and we'll start tomorrow night. I want it operational by supper time."

"You wanna run it out of the van?" Jefferson asked, making notes.

"Yes, when you get the papers for the judge, bring them to me at my place and I'll sign them. I'm going home now. There are things to do."

"I'll bet," Jefferson said with a grin.

"Knock it off, Pancho," Donovan said wearily.

Jefferson was not put off. "Nail her once for me, boss," he said as Donovan slipped out the door.

YOU CAN'T TEACH A MONKEY TO PLAY THE OBOE

"I'm gonna wring their necks," Donovan growled, working with a brush and a bottle of Lysol to clean the pigeon shit off his bedroom windowsill.

"Shoot one and leave the body there. That'll discourage the others," Marcie suggested.

"Nah. Pigeons aren't smart enough to take the hint. Now, if the goddam turtle had only worked out . . ."

"Snapping turtles were meant to sit in ponds and eat ducks, not sit on windowsills and eat pigeons. You can't teach a monkey to play the oboe. Why don't you do as I suggested and put him in a fish tank and feed him hamburger meat? I'll run down to the Woolworth's on Seventy-ninth tomorrow and buy you a fish tank, if you promise to pay me back."

"Maybe he was pissed at me for tying his tail to a chair. I was just trying to keep him from falling out."

"Donovan," she said, "you're an incorrigible fuckup. Let me think of a way of getting rid of your flock for you."

"You can do that?"

"I can do anything."

Donovan finished scrubbing the sill and closed the window. Marcie had on a maroon jogging suit, and was taping a wire to her left arm. The wire came out from under her sleeve and terminated in an unobtrusive-looking wristwatch. She pulled the sleeve down to cover the wire.

"There. The mike is in the watch. The transmitter is in the hood. That's why I got a jogging suit with such a large hood. The antenna runs down my left side."

"Earphone?"

"Here." She pulled a tiny earphone from under the neckline and pressed it into her right ear. "You won't be able to see it after dark."

Donovan nodded. "Okay, let's try it out. Go into the park by the stairs to the south of the Soldiers and Sailors Monument. Go down to the lower mall and jog south to the handball courts, then north to the tennis courts. Stop there and introduce yourself to the kindly looking Mexican who works at the place. He's the only civilian who knows we're using you as a decoy to draw the killer out. Then jog back down to the monument and come home. Keep the channel open the whole time. Dismissed."

"You really like this, don't you?" she said. "You think you're General Patton or something."

"So what if I do? Nowhere does it say I can't enjoy my work. Now, you have a cop by the monument, another at the handball courts, and a third with my Mexican friend. The wino you'll find sacked out on a bench on the lower mall halfway through your run is also one of my men."

"Do they all have radios?"

"Yeah. You'll be the most looked-after broad since Lillie Langtry. I'll run the show from up here, where I have a pretty good view of the entire route."

"Can't you get someone else to work the radio up here? I'd like to have you closer."

"Sorry. I can't be seen with you in the park at night. It might blow the whole thing. It's bad enough I had to tell Gomez about it."

"Who's he?"

"The only tout who never picked a winning horse. You'll love him. On your way."

Marcie kissed Donovan on the cheek. "I'm putting my ass on the line for you," she said. "You had better make it worth my while."

THE TEST WORKED PERFECTLY

Donovan imagined himself directing a tank battle against the Afrika Korps in Tunisia. He clipped a high-gain antenna to his newly scoured windowsill and, sipping a beer, directed the test run.

Marcie's transmitter worked perfectly. Serious joggers routinely check their times on wristwatches, so there was no problem in bringing the mike to her lips. When she finished her circuit, Donovan impulsively ordered her to stop and sit on the low stone wall where they had both sat earlier in the day.

Donovan wanted her to spend enough time in the park to be noticed. It might take weeks of daily runs, but he meant to establish her in the killer's mind as a young, vaguely dark-skinned girl who frequented the park in the late afternoon and early evening.

He watched her as she sat shaking the kinks out of her legs and stretching her arms. She was clear enough in his binoculars, but only because she was near two street lamps. Donovan promised himself to get some night vision gear for the next evening's run. As he wondered where he could lay his hands on an Army Sniperscope, the sound of his doorbell ringing was infuriating.

"Come in!" he yelled.

The doorbell rang again. The front door was some distance from his bedroom.

"I can't come to the door!" he bellowed, louder this time.

The door opened and closed, and he heard footsteps in the hall. It would have to be Jefferson with the wiretap application.

"In the bedroom," Donovan said, still watching Marcie.

"Bill?"

The voice belonged to Jack. Donovan spun around, saw the face of one of his prime suspects, and his heart sank.

"Donovan?"

Marcie's voice was clear in the loudspeaker, and Donovan returned his attention to her.

"Yeah, babe?"

"Nothing going on. Hey . . . that cop who looks like a wino? I think he *is* a wino. He hasn't moved since I've been here."

A muffled 'fuck you' came over the airwaves.

"I train 'em personally," Donovan said. "Come on in, Marcie. This is enough for one night. You by the monument, you got her in sight?"

"Got her, lieutenant," was the reply.

"She's yours. I'm going off the air."

Donovan put aside his microphone and binoculars and turned to Jack.

"Hi," he said with a sigh.

"I barged in on something. I'm sorry."

Jack looked both confused and contrite. It was not, after all, his fault.

"You've obviously surmised that I have a policewoman working undercover in the park. I'll have to trust you to keep your mouth shut."

"Unh . . . of course," Jack said uncertainly.

"Not a word, not about the girl or anything. Got it?"

"Yeah, I got it. Look, Bill, I dug this up for you. It may be some help."

He walked across the room and gave Donovan a sheaf of Xerox copies.

"I got this from a book in the university library. It's a pretty good description of Haitian ritual. I can interpret the scientific jargon for you if you like."

"Sure," Donovan said. "Get yourself a beer. You know where the kitchen is. I'll send my boys home and meet you in the living room."

BARON SAMEDI

"He's the one I want," Donovan said, perking up at last when after a long discourse on the finer points of voodoo, Jack came upon the name of the god of death.

"Baron Samedi, it says here, is both comic and arrogant. The matter of death seems to be a joke with him. He's frequently seen wearing a cutaway coat, top hat, and carrying a cane. There's also an element of vulgarity involved. You know, dirty jokes."

"You talk like he's a real person," Marcie said. Just-showered, she wore a t-shirt and cutoff jeans and looked wonderful.

"He is, in a way. The celebrants affect his manner and sing his favorite dirty songs. The one celebrant who becomes possessed *does* become him."

"Could he kill under those circumstances?" Donovan asked.

"If he did, he would have no recollection of it afterward," Jack replied.

Marcie yawned and said, "I'm going to send out for Chinese food. Anybody care to join me?"

Donovan raised his hand, but Jack said no. "I have to grade some papers. Why don't you read the rest of the article. It should give you a pretty good idea what's going on."

Marcie excused herself, padding off on bare feet into the vastness of Donovan's apartment.

"So that's the girl you used to live with," Jack said. "She's stunning."

"Thanks," Donovan said, leading the way to the door. "Is this serious?"

"It's a serious police investigation, so I'll ask you again to keep your mouth shut. Only two civilians know about it, so I can always find the loudmouth if word of it gets out."

"You have nothing to worry about from me," Jack said.

"Okay," Donovan said, giving Jack a slap on the back. "Thanks for bringing me the article. If Baron Samedi shows up, I'll tell him I didn't hear it from you."

When Jack was gone, Marcie came back into the living room with a paper menu from the local Szechuan restaurant. "I'll have braised green beans with bamboo shoots," she said, then sniffed, "I take it you're still eating chop suey?"

"I really blew it," Donovan said. "I shouldn't have let Jack know about you."

"Don't worry about it. He looks harmless. His fingernails

were manicured, and he doesn't appear to have a muscle in
his body. Besides, he seems anxious to help."

"Or anxious to have suspicion shifted away from the
Aztec and Pawnee angles."

"You're too suspicious," Marcie said. "Forget the case for
the rest of the evening and tell me what you want to eat."

"Sweet and sour pork," he replied. "I'm trying to elevate
my taste."

"Yeah? Well, you blew that too."

A HOPELESS JUMBLE OF BULLSHIT

That was how Donovan characterized the rituals apparently
involved in the three killings.

"This is no more Haitian than it is Aztec, Pawnee, or
Martian so far as I can tell. It's a hopeless jumble of bullshit."

"Finish your food."

"I ate all I want."

"There's a little left. If you don't have it, I'll feed it to the
pigeons on your windowsill."

"I'll eat it," Donovan said quickly. "But *really*, babe, the
rituals are missing all sorts of things a true voodoo ceremony
would have—a shrine, an altar, dancing, singing, drums, just
to mention a few."

"All the things that would require more than one celebrant," Marcie observed.

"Yeah, I know. I could be all wet chasing these Haitians
and Pawnees all over the West Side. On the other hand,
Camelia Rodriguez *was* exactly the right age, she *had* been
treated like a princess for months, corn kernels *were* involved, and, my God, I've even got a tribe of Indians! As

well as Haitians who are *known* to practice voodoo. How much more can you ask for?"

"A smoking pistol, my dear Donovan, a smoking pistol. You just sit back and eat your dinner. Sooner or later, I'll catch your killer for you."

A GOOD LINE OF WORK

"You ever think of goin' into TV repair, lieutenant?" Jefferson asked, fiddling idly with the volume knob on the tape deck before him.

"No."

"There's a lot of money to be made."

"Listen, it took me until the age of reason to figure out how to turn the goddam TV on. Electronics ain't exactly my cup of tea."

By way of emphasizing the point, Donovan wadded up a piece of paper and bounced it off a monitor which sat alongside the tape deck. The back of the old van had been turned into a grubby and cramped but efficient spy center, with a wiretap running into the below-street junction box and a TV camera trained on the front door of Patrino's. Wires sprouted like weeds from an array of electronic components which Jefferson seemed to know by heart but which Donovan called "boxes" and distinguished by size and shape.

Patrino's was slightly larger than Riley's and owned by Italians, not Jews. But it had a clientele that was almost exclusively black and Hispanic. The clientele was so solidly nonwhite that Donovan would have been as out-of-place as an elephant. Jefferson was too well-dressed and, anyway, needed to run the machines. Donovan drank coffee and watched the front door of the bar as it appeared on the TV monitor. Patrino's was well-lit, distinguished by an il-luminated plastic façade on which were the words "cocktail lounge" and a pair of dancing champagne glasses that spouted bubbles. The bar stood between a Chinese grocery store and a tiny and dismal dry cleaners.

"What time is it?" Donovan asked.

"Eight forty. You been here an hour. The guy hasn't showed up yet, so you wanna go home?"

"No. One failure a day isn't enough for me. I got to stay here until this one falls on its face too."

"So you didn't pick up on anything in your second run with Marcie. What the hell do you expect? And it's only been a couple days since the last murder. The others were all a week apart."

"I know," Donovan conceded. "I want to get it over with. Camelia's funeral mass is tomorrow. I kinda wanted to bring her family good news."

"We could get lucky tonight," Jefferson said.

"Sure," Donovan said, with no enthusiasm.

"Go home."

"I have to be here to spot the guy."

"I'll see him when he shows up."

"What? You don't even know what he looks like."

"I can spot a Haitian a mile off. You know how *you* can always tell an Englishman? A Haitian doesn't walk the same as a brother, and most of the time doesn't dress as good as a Puerto Rican, if you can imagine that."

"Just the same I'll stay," Donovan said. "It's getting near nine o'clock. Wait . . . there he is. That's the guy."

Donovan tapped his finger against the image on the monitor. The dark-skinned man stopped in front of Patrino's, lit a cigarette while looking around, then ducked inside.

"Hit the horn," Donovan snapped.

Jefferson lunged into the front of the van and blew a long blast on the horn by way of telling Detective Munoz, inside Patrino's enjoying the benefits of saloon stakeouts, that the suspect had entered.

"He's inside at eight forty-seven," Jefferson said, repositioning himself in front of the bank of equipment.

"I give him three minutes to buy a drink before he makes a call," Donovan said.

"We have a take," Jefferson said, rewinding the videotape. "Stand by for instant replay."

He played back the image of the man and froze it. Leaning forward, Donovan smiled at last. "That's him."

Jefferson ran the tape ahead to where he left off and started it again. He used the van's radio to tell the two stake-out teams parked on Ninety-ninth and Columbus to be ready to roll. If he followed true to form, the Haitian wouldn't be in the barroom long.

At exactly 8:54 P.M. the phone in Patrino's rang, and outside in the van, Jefferson's automatic phone equipment switched on. As Jefferson made notes, Donovan leaned forward, straining to hear every sound. The conversation he heard was short:

"Patrino's."

"Is Charlie Dubay there?"

"Who?"

"Charlie Dubay."

There was a lot of background noise as the bartender called out Dubay's name and the Haitian took the phone.

"Hello?"

"It's me. We're leaving Weehawken now."

"How many you got?"

"Six. We'll meet you at the same place as last time."

"When?"

"Ten."

"Okay."

Jefferson looked up at his boss. "Six what? Kilos?"

"Probably chickens to slaughter," said Donovan. "It's too much to hope that it might be six celebrants for a ritual killing."

NIGHT BOAT FROM WEEHAWKEN

It was only ten in the evening, but Donovan felt as if he'd been up all night. As he and his men followed Charlie Dubay from Patrino's to a station wagon on Columbus and from there around half the West Side, it became increasingly obvious that while Dubay was up to something illegal, that something wasn't ritual killing. The Haitian went through the expected maneuvers which failed to shake the policemen tailing him, then at last drove up the ramp onto the southbound lanes of the West Side Highway.

He drove south to the turnoff for Ninety-sixth Street, took the ramp to get off the highway, then pulled to the side of the road at a disabled vehicle area on the edge of a little-used part of the elaborate clover leaf. That area was also right by the edge of the Hudson River, at the north end of a short walkway and river overlook. A short metal fence and six feet of large rocks separated Manhattan Island from the water.

Intensely disappointed, Donovan took up a position on the grass a hundred yards north of Dubay.

"The son of a bitch has found the only way to get into Riverside Park despite our curfew, and with a car to boot."

"It can't be helped," Jefferson said. "We can't fence off the whole place and do it effectively. If we did, the killer couldn't get into the park, either."

"I wonder," Donovan said idly, unaware of the portent of his words.

"Does it really take an hour to get here from Weehawken by boat?"

"With the tide at full ebb, yeah. With a current of five knots and an old boat that only makes six knots, it could take more than an hour to get here from Weehawken."

"It's got to be grass. The guy is bringing in grass from Haiti in pound lots. Probably gettin' it from the sailors who come into the Banana Terminal at Weehawken. I don't know why I never thought of grass in pound lots."

Donovan shook his head. "It's not grass. It's *sailors* he's bringing in. Illegal aliens. Immigration has been wondering how the fuck so many Haitians have been managing to jump ship in Weehawken. John Flaherty has had men watching the streets around the Banana Terminal for the past couple of months."

"So they sneak up with an old boat and bring 'em to our side of the river," Jefferson said, joining his boss in sad shakes of the head. "What a fuckin' bring-down. I don't believe I've been breaking my balls to arrest a goddam bunch of illegal aliens."

"Console yourself with arresting Dubay for killing Peter Geffrard . . ."

"Who worked with his old man to sell tickets into the U.S.," Jefferson concluded.

"You got it."

"And got killed when Dubay thought he was spilling the beans to you."

"Ditto," Donovan said.

"We ain't never gonna get our hands on Geffrard's old man."

"Somebody will get him eventually. Men in his line of work seldom make it to retirement age. Are all our guys in place?"

"Let me check," Jefferson said, and did so, working with his walkie-talkie set on quiet talk. There were a few cars on the West Side Highway, and the rushing of their tires on the concrete nearly hid the putt-putting of an old boat engine. Donovan could see an old launch, perhaps forty feet long, chugging valiantly toward shore, fighting the swift current as well as the need borne of secrecy to stay in the swift channel to the center of the river. Dubay appeared to grow more and more nervous as the launch drew nearer. He repeatedly looked around him and lit one cigarette after another, tossing the half-smoked butts into the water.

"Everyone's ready," Jefferson reported.

"No one moves until I give the word. I want to wait until they're all on shore and Dubay has, so to speak, taken delivery. I want Dubay personally. I don't like the idea he killed a guy I drank with."

The launch approached the rocky Manhattan shore line and Dubay, thinking himself alone, waved it in. He climbed to a position astride the four-foot metal fence, caught a rope thrown from the launch, and tied it to the rail. Quickly, seven men scrambled up over the rocks, climbed the fence, and stood in a small clump by the station wagon.

"Now!" Donovan snapped, and Jefferson touched his lips to his radio and said, "Go! Go! Go!"

Off in the distance, a bullhorn barked orders to freeze, while hand-held floodlights lit the scene.

The newly arrived Haitians huddled together, uncomprehending but frightened. The man who had piloted the boat dived back into it, while Dubay started running north. He pulled a black automatic from under his belt and fired two rounds at one of the floodlights. There was answering fire from Donovan's men, and Jefferson positioned himself behind a small tree.

Donovan pulled his .38 and waited. Dubay was looking behind, not in front, running slowly because of the slope. Donovan took aim.

"Police! Freeze!"

Dubay whirled, saw the lieutenant and fired. Donovan fired a single shot which caught the Haitian in the middle, folded him like a slip of paper, and dropped him to the ground.

IT'S QUARTER TO THREE

"There ain't no one here except you and me," she told him.

"I hope not," he said, tossing off his jacket and shoulder holster and flopping down on the couch.

Marcie went into the kitchen and came back with a beer. She popped the top and handed him the can, wiping the spray on his shirt. She wore nothing.

Marcie draped herself over the arms of an old easy chair across the room from him and asked, "How'd it go tonight?"

"We can forget the Haitian angle to the case. Geffrard was bringing illegal aliens into the country, and his father was certainly a part of the deal. It was a nice scheme. The old man's police force made life intolerable for the poor bastards in Haiti, then he sold them entry into the United States. The manager at this end was a Haitian named Dubay, who was also Geffrard's murderer. Geffrard was killed with a 9mm automatic. The bullets match Dubay's gun."

"And you got Dubay?"

"He's in the hands of the Lord now," Donovan said, with mock solemnity.

Marcie's eyes blazed, and she swung her feet to the floor. "You killed him?" she asked.

"Yeah," Donovan said, recognizing her sexual longing and feeling at once both embarrassed and thrilled by it.

"You remember the last time you killed someone? When we were living together? What it did to you?"

Of course Donovan remembered. He had felt big, powerful, overwhelming . . . an animal. He wanted everything, took most of it, and regretted it afterwards. "I felt bad about that for a long time," he said.

Marcie went to Donovan and draped herself across his lap. "Feel bad about it," she said, "in the morning."

The Catholic Church of the Sacred Heart was an old, simple church on Amsterdam Avenue near 104th Street. If its spire was grimy and some of its stained glass shattered by rocks, the church was roomy inside. Even so, the Hispanic community packed it to the rafters for the funeral mass of Camelia Rodriguez.

A row of hearses and limousines, paid for by neighborhood contributions, stood in the street, which volunteers had swept for the occasion. A crowd of several hundred mourners was held back from the church entrance by police barricades. Two television camera crews, kept down the block by police, filmed the proceedings.

During the mass, Donovan stood alone at the back of the church. He hadn't set foot in a church in years except for funerals, and had come to associate religion with death. He muttered a Hail Mary and as much of the Lord's Prayer as he could remember, and waited until it was over. As the mourners filed out, the family walked behind them. Rosie kept her eyes cast down, and if she saw Donovan, didn't acknowledge him. But her father did look at Donovan. Their eyes met, the elder Rodriguez smiled bravely, and touched Donovan's arm as he passed.

Donovan waited until the procession was past, then followed it into the street. There were tears from the Cubans and other neighborhood Hispanics outside, and flowers. The TV news crews panned from the weeping Rodriguez family as the cars drove away to Donovan, standing on the church steps. Before he had time to get away, he found himself staring into a camera and saying, "We're still working on the case, but at the moment we have nothing new to tell you."

That meant he was left with Johnny Silver Shoes, Jack, or X, the unknown. Coming on top of the funeral, it was a depressing thought.

"LOOK FOR CLUES, LOOK FOR CLUES," SHE SAID

"Forget about looking for people," Marcie went on. "You're pushing forty, slugger. Your brain is starting to atrophy. So look for clues while your eyes are still working."

Marcie was in the bedroom, strapping her radio gear to her body prior to putting on her jogging suit. Donovan was sorry he had to veto a tennis outfit similar to the one Camelia wore, but all Marcie's electronics simply wouldn't fit under one like that. Besides, she had too much of a figure to be convincing as a fifteen-year-old. She had, after all, spent the past two years playing a high-class hooker in midtown. Even with radios, batteries, and wires strapped to it, Marcie's body was delightful. Donovan found himself getting horned up, and, embarrassed, left the bedroom.

"I have to set up the Sniperscope," he mumbled.

Donovan got all the way down the long hall of the apartment and halfway across the foyer when he heard the plain-

tive sound of his door buzzer not working. It broke periodically, one such occasion being the day before. Marcie had
promised to fix it, but hadn't gotten around to the job.
Shaking his head, Donovan pulled open the door to find
himself staring at Rosie.

She was dressed in her old jeans and a t-shirt on which
was emblazoned the logo of the Broadway show *Evita*. She
looked contrite, a bit sheepish, and smiled faintly. "Hello,
William."

"Unh . . . hi."

"Are you busy?"

"I'm getting ready for a surveillance, but I have some
time. Come in."

He led her into the living room and was about to excuse
himself so he could warn Marcie, but she took him by the
hands. "William, I want to say how sorry I am for treating
you so badly. I was a little crazy."

"Forget it."

"No. I blamed you for Camelia's death, and it was wrong.
My father bawled me out good and proper for it."

"I blamed myself," Donovan said.

She looked about to cry. He hugged her, and touched her
hair softly, then broke away.

"I want to talk to you," he said, with some urgency, "but
I have to do something. Can you wait a second?"

She nodded, and just then Marcie strode into the living
room.

"Donovan, can you hook up the earphone cable for me?
Oh . . . I'm sorry."

She was wearing jogging pants, but no top. She turned
her back. Blushing, Donovan hooked up the wire in question.

"Rosie, this is Marcia Barnes," he said.

"That's *Sergeant* Barnes," Marcie added. "I didn't know you were here. I can't hook up all this junk by myself." And she disappeared back down the hall.

Rosie was looking down, expressionless. "I'd better go," she said.

"Wait a minute. I want to explain something."

"You don't have to."

"Yes, I do. Marcie and I used to live together, which accounts for the degree of informality. She's here because she's the best undercover policewoman in the city. Every night she puts on a jogging suit and hangs around the park, trying to lure out of hiding the man who killed your sister."

Rosie sighed. "Okay. I see. Look, William, I never demanded fidelity."

Donovan was frustrated and felt his temper rising. "Dammit, the fact that Marcie and I used to have a thing going is beside the point. She's here to catch a murderer. Once she gets that radio working, she's going down into the park to risk her goddam life!"

"I know . . . I just . . . well, I said what I came here to say. I have to go to work. George has been filling in for me the past couple of nights."

"Can I see you later?"

"Sure," she said, and allowed him to press a kiss on her passive lips. "Come in near to closing time."

When she was gone, Marcie came back. "Oh, baby, I'm *sorry,*" she said. "I knew I should have fixed that doorbell. Do you think you can patch things up with her?"

Donovan was disgusted with almost every aspect of his life. "I never thought it would last forever," he said forlornly.

"Did you want it to?"

"Come on," he said, "let's get to work."

CLOSING TIME

At closing time, Riley's was deserted except for two custom-ers. Big Harold was drinking shots and beer and watching "Rat Patrol," which Rosie had switched on in anticipation of Donovan's arrival. The other customer was known only as Doc, a nickname which would have been insufferably cute had he not at one time been a doctor.

The doctor had been a successful general practitioner with an office on Riverside Drive during the thirties, forties, and fifties. But during that last-mentioned decade his wife developed colonic cancer and Doc went flat broke paying her medical bills. By the time she died, weighing seventy pounds and shriveled like an autumn leaf, he had turned to performing abortions to keep up with expenses. In 1957 one of his patients died.

Doc's license to practice was revoked and he served eigh-teen months for manslaughter. It was during that time that his wife passed away. The doctor spent the sixties and seven-ties in an alcoholic stupor that increased by the day. At the beginning of the eighties it seemed that nothing short of the grave would spare him from putting in another decade be-hind the bottle.

Donovan felt embarrassed and a bit guilty in Doc's pres-ence. His father had been the arresting officer who sent the pitiable old man to Sing Sing. Fortunately, on this evening when Donovan came in, Doc had gone into the back room and was passed out in a booth, his white hair spilling across the torn vinyl seat.

Rosie was drunk. She had been hitting the Cuba Libres pretty hard. Donovan could see it the moment he walked in and sat down next to Harold. "Hi," she said, opening a bottle of Schmidt's and unsteadily placing it on the bar.

Harold leaned toward Donovan, squinted, formed the fingers of one hand into an imaginary pistol, and said "bang." It was a gesture he employed when he didn't like a stranger. It was a warning to watch your step or your head would be broken.

"What the fuck did I do?" Donovan asked.

"Just kidding," the big man laughed. "Here . . . let me buy you a beer."

"It's on the house," Rosie said. "Anyway, it's closing time and I can't take money. Watch the store, would you, William? I have to turn off the lights in the back."

"What about him?" Donovan asked, indicating the form of the doctor slumped over in back.

"I'll take him home," Harold said. "He lives in my building."

"I didn't know he lived in One Seventy," Donovan said, meaning 170 Riverside, the building next to his.

"That's where he lives. I take him home all the time. He doesn't like me, but I do it anyway."

The janitor finished his beer, gathered up the old man, and without another word carried him out the door.

Donovan sipped his beer while Rosie finished closing up shop. When she locked the door and burglar's gates behind them, Donovan took her hand. "I'll walk you home," he said.

"Okay."

They walked along Broadway. There was no traffic, not even on Eighty-sixth Street.

"Any luck tonight?" she asked.

"None. Absolutely none. Marcie hung around that park long enough to be seen, and there wasn't so much as a nibble. Then again, this is only the third night we've been at it."

"She's staying at your place, isn't she?"

Donovan nodded.

"Then you'd better get right back."

"Marcie is a former lover and an old friend. I don't owe her anything but friendship."

"Aren't you expected?"

"Nope, nor will I be missed. She's a big girl, Rosie, a black belt in karate, and a dedicated cop. She can take care of herself both physically and emotionally."

"She's very beautiful, too," Rosie noted.

"That she is."

"How come you broke up?"

"She's an East Side girl. She enjoys life in the fast lane. You know, the Russian Tea Room and roller disco. When she's with me, she's slumming. After a very short time we get on each other's nerves."

Rosie took Donovan's arm and walked with him up Broadway to Ninety-sixth, and east to Amsterdam. Outside her apartment door, she turned and faced him. "I got drunk tonight because I didn't know how I'd react when you showed up. I didn't know if I wanted to see you again."

"And how *do* you feel?" Donovan asked.

Rosie took both his hands, squeezed them and said, "I want you to stay with me tonight. Will you?"

Donovan smiled, and went with her into the apartment.

CROIX DE GUERRE

The phone rang half a dozen times before Marcie picked it up. It was dark in the bedroom, and she yawned a "hello" into the receiver.

"Sergeant Barnes?"

"Yes."

"Is Lieutenant Donovan there?"

"Just a second." She covered the mouthpiece, patted his side of the bed, then called his name several times. "It doesn't look like it."

"This is Officer Pellici. I'm down by the Soldiers and Sailors Monument. You better get down here."

"What's up?" Marcie asked, swinging her feet off the bed.

"Somebody set a fire down in the park. It's in the shape of a big goddam cross. Look out the window."

Marcie took the phone to the window. The fiery cross was deep in the park, on the softball and frisbee area near the lower mall. It was near the spot where she loitered after her nightly runs.

"Christ! Okay, I'm on my way."

"Do you know where the lieutenant is?"

"No. Wait, he's probably with Rosie. What's her last name? Rodriguez, I think. The sister of the last victim. I don't know where she lives."

"I'll try to find him," Pellici said.

Marcie pulled on a pair of jeans and one of Donovan's sweatshirts which was far too big. It hung halfway to her knees, and she had to buckle her Sam Browne over it, so she looked like a Mexican bandit. Running as fast as she could, she joined Pellici and two other uniformed cops at the Eighty-ninth Street entrance. From there, the fiery cross was much bigger than it looked from Donovan's apartment.

"Did you find Donovan?" she asked.

"Not yet. Do you know how many people there are named Rodriguez in the phone book?"

Marcie drew her revolver and checked it. "We can't wait for him. Let's go."

"Maybe we better get more guys down here," Pellici said.

"For God's sake, man, this could be our best chance. Leave one man here and come with me."

And she started down the steps, with Pellici and another cop behind her.

The asphalt paths snaked down the steep hill, and once again the park lights were out. Marcie went straight cross-country, picking her way from tree to tree, her .38 in front of her. The two other cops followed, and the site of the burning approached.

The air was filled with the acrid smell of burned oil. The dirt and tamped-down grass of the softball and frisbee area were marked with a Greek cross thirty feet in both dimensions. The flames, initially four feet high, were only a foot high when Marcie reached the edge of the cross.

She skirted it slowly and looked around in the fire light. She expected to find a body at the center of the cross or somewhere within it, but there was none. Marcie and Officer Pellici exchanged puzzled looks, and then she saw movement across the lower mall. A tall, hulking figure stood by the short stone wall which separated the lower mall from a grassy shoulder and then the West Side Highway. Marcie raised her gun, and Pellici did the same.

"Police! Freeze!"

The figure stood stock-still for a second, as if making up its mind. Then it dived over the wall.

Marcie fired two rounds. The slugs tore chunks of concrete from the wall on which Donovan and she had sat when she first entered the case.

Marcie ran across the lower mall and looked over the wall. There was nothing, no movement at all. There was some traffic on the highway, but the headlights picked up no motion on the grassy shoulder. Marcie vaulted the wall and

ran quickly to the lip of the highway. Perhaps he had es-
caped along it. No such luck.

Pellici joined her. "Did you see him?"

Marcie shook her head and holstered her pistol.

They walked back across the shoulder. At a spot a few
yards south of where they had vaulted the wall, the grass
dipped down to reveal an ancient iron door set in the stone
face of the wall. The door looked as though it hadn't been
open since the park was built in the 1930s.

A bleary-eyed Donovan peered down at Marcie from the
top of the wall.

"Jesus, I can't leave you alone for five minutes, can I?" he
said.

MAYBE VAN DANIKEN PUT IT THERE

"You know him? The guy who says the Indians drew things on the ground to guide UFOs in for a landing? Maybe he did it."

"Are we on Indians again?" Marcie asked. "Come on, Donovan, you're just pissed that I dragged you out of the sack."

Once again, the spotlights from squad cars illuminated a broad section of Riverside Park. The fiery cross had gone out on its own, and evidence teams crawled across it, taking samples of charred and uncharred soil.

"I can't say for sure until tomorrow, lieutenant," one technician reported, "but it looks like ordinary home heating oil to me."

"How much of it would you need to build a fire this size and keep it going for half an hour?"

"Let's see . . . two struts sixty feet by two feet? Ten gallons minimum, and twenty is more like it."

"Where's the can?" Donovan asked.

"He must have taken it with him," Marcie said.

"Do you expect me to believe that a man of considerable

stature, carrying a twenty-gallon oil can, ran down the West
Side Highway without anyone noticing?"

"It's five in the morning, Donovan."

"You never heard of commuters?"

"Okay," she said with an exasperated sigh, "there were
some cars, but all in the southbound lanes, and that's the
other side of the highway. It took us three, maybe five
minutes to get our guys onto the northbound lane. No,
make it ten minutes. The northbound access ramp is all the
way down at Seventy-ninth. The killer could have run all
the way up to Ninety-sixth, through the underpass, and
halfway to Broadway in that time."

"Uh huh," Donovan said. "Now show me where you
were standing when you took a shot at him."

Marcie did as she was told. When she was in her place and
Donovan in the killer's, they reenacted the shooting and
pursuit. When Marcie and Pellici got over the wall and to
the edge of the highway, Donovan was gone.

"Where'd he go?" Pellici asked.

Marcie turned to see Donovan lounging in the old doorway, looking pleased as punch.

"I looked there," she said.

"When?"

"After I ran to the highway."

"If I were him and had the key to this door, I would have
been inside by then."

"I was no more than thirty seconds behind him," Marcie
protested.

"And if I had the door *open* and waiting for me to duck
inside? I'd duck inside, wait for you and Pellici to give up and
go back over the wall, then let myself out and escape along
the highway. You were up fiddling with the fiery cross for
twenty minutes at least, and no one was watching this door."

"Come on, Donovan, that door hasn't been opened in years."

"Hasn't it? Let's find out. Get some lights down here and we'll have a look at the lock."

"What the hell's in there, Donovan?"

"Open the door," he said, "and we'll find out."

THE CURSE OF AMON-RA

"I feel like Howard Carter opening King Tut's tomb," Donovan said as police technicians set up the portable flood-lights they had used so many times of late.

"Don't romanticize, Donovan. It's probably the room where the workmen eat their sandwiches."

"What workmen? Rolland says that nobody ever goes in or out of these doors. Well, nobody he knows of, and he knows all the workmen."

"That's right," the Mexican nodded, agreeable even when hauled out of bed by the police at five in the morning. "This was supposed to be a pumping station for the sewer system, but it was never started up. There is a little room to the left of it which has a lot of Con Ed equipment in it."

"What kind of equipment?" Donovan asked.

"You know . . . the power cables for the park. This part of it, anyway."

"When was the last time you were in there?"

"Two . . . no, three years ago. The Con Ed guys were fixing something and I stuck my head in."

"Have they been back?"

"I don't think so."

"Is there any other way into those rooms?"

Again Gomez gave a negative reply. Donovan nodded and, the lights in place, stepped up to the door and peered intently at the lock, the hinges, and the vines covering the iron bars on the door. Using a pocket screwdriver, he poked the sliding edges of the top hinge, then turned to Marcie, Gomez, and the crowd of technicians waiting for him to have his look.

"The lock is new but has been made to look old," he said. "The lack of rust around the sliding edges of the hinges seems to show that the door has been opened recently. And the vines are crushed on the rightmost bar, just where a man would grasp it to pull the door open."

He stepped back and waited while the experts confirmed his opinion, one of them adding, "The face of the lock has been painted with dark varnish to make it look old. It's a new series Yale lock, lieutenant. I have the master. You want the door open?"

"Yeah."

Donovan drew his pistol and flattened himself against the wall just to the right of the door. Marcie crouched beside him, her .38 held in both hands before her. The technician selected one key from a large ring and slipped it into the lock.

"Now," Donovan ordered.

The door swung open as Donovan held his breath. It was dark inside, and there was no sound. Donovan stood stock-still for a long ten seconds before moving swiftly into the room.

The room was absolutely empty. The floor was swept, as the murder sites had been. In the air were two scents, home heating oil and candle wax. After a quick check of the room and the adjoining compartment, Donovan had technicians

brought in and the lights switched on. As half-a-dozen policemen from the evidence team swarmed over the underground chambers, Marcie holstered her revolver.

"So much for barricaded suspects," she said. "It's too bad,
too. I was kind of hoping he'd be in here. Then we could .
get it over with and I could get back to living on the East
Side. You've heard of the East Side, haven't you, Donovan?
That's where civilization is."

"He was here," Donovan said.

"You don't know that."

"Sure I do. There's the lock, and the fact that the door has
been opened recently. And what about the smell? Candles,
which we know he uses, and oil?"

"The floor's been swept recently, lieutenant," a voice
said. "I'm getting brush marks on the floor. And look at that
ceiling. It's covered with cobwebs and dust. That stuff has
to fall regularly. Compare this floor with the one in the Con
Ed room. That floor's as dirty as you would expect."

"See," Donovan told Marcie.

"There's more," another voice said. "You wanna come in
here, lieutenant?"

Donovan followed the voice into the small, adjoining
room, where a bank of the Consolidated Edison Company's
equipment occupied one wall. A technician stood by the
main panel, the switching point for the electricity running
through that section of Riverside Park. He held an electrical
probe, its tip pointing out terminals where red and green
wires joined their mates.

"This is one spot where you can disrupt the street lights
in the park between the tennis courts and, say, Seventy-
second. Somebody's been fucking around in here. These
terminals have been played with a lot."

"Explaining the way the lights go off when our murderer decides to stage an event," Donovan said. "Thank you, officer."

Donovan went back into the main room which, filled up with policemen, seemed nowhere near as cavernous as when Donovan first entered it. Gomez had come in as well, and was by the east wall, leaning against the end of the six-foot sluice pipe where it stuck six inches out of the wall.

"What's this?" Donovan asked, patting the heavy iron cover which screwed onto the end of the sluice.

"The sewer pipe, what else?"

"That's a big pipe."

"There's a lot of shit in New York," Gomez said, smiling at his own witticism. The cover was printed, in raised letters, with the legend "City of New York, Dept. of Water & Sewers."

"Where does this come from?" Donovan asked.

The answer was shrugs all around.

"It was supposed to go to the treatment plant up on a hundred and thirty-seventh," Gomez said. "This here room was to be a pumping station. But it never happened."

Donovan nodded. "Take off the cover," he said.

"Come on, lieutenant," a technician protested, "that thing's got to weigh three hundred pounds."

Donovan gave the man a withering glance and, before too long, three men had the cover off and on the floor.

"I make it two hundred pounds," one of them said.

"A bit much for one man," Marcie observed.

"Unh huh," Donovan grunted, peering into the huge pipe with the help of a flashlight. The inside was damp, and the slightest sound echoed, seemingly, for miles.

Donovan pulled his head back out. "Put the cover back."

Marcie took his arm and led him out into the growing daylight. "Come on, baby, let's go home. That is, if duty and Rosie are done with you."

"He used that room. I can feel it."

"Okay, he hid in there until we stopped looking, and then let himself out and went away. What of it? The place is blown now as a cover for him."

"This whole thing? The fiery cross set almost under my window. No body, but a big invitation to come down here. And you tell me the guy was hanging around, as if waiting for me to show up? This whole thing is aimed at me, I tell you. I'm more convinced of it than ever."

"Donovan," she sighed, "with all due respect, you're not that important."

"To somebody I am," he maintained.

"To me, baby. Let's go home." And she took his arm and pulled him away.

ENGLISH MUFFINS AND MARMALADE

Donovan went home to Rosie instead. The fiery cross in the park had interrupted them before the *fait* could be *accompli*'d, and Donovan felt she deserved better than another apology.

They made love for the usual amount of time, then fell asleep for several hours. Donovan woke up at ten in the morning, to the delicious odor of butter and English muffins. She had learned quickly that there was more to cuisine than refried beans and jalapeño peppers.

"I'm glad you came back last night," she said.

"Me too."

"I worry about you, William. You know, I *believe* you

when you say that these terrible things are aimed at you. I don't understand why, but I believe."

"Some sin out of my past, maybe. I wish I could remember what it is. Anyway, either because of past sins or the notoriety I've been getting lately, the killer is aiming his efforts at me. Which means he has a highly developed sense of humor. Sick, but highly developed. He has managed to drop enough hints about Haitian and Pawnee ritual to get me running all over the place tracking down phony leads. I imagine he's enjoying the spectacle."

"When you say 'phony leads,' do you mean that Johnny Silver Shoes is innocent?" Rosie asked.

"I think so, but I'm not sure. After I find out where he was last night I'll have a better idea."

"And your friend Jack?"

"The same."

"I hope you're right. Johnny seems like an all right kind of guy, after all."

"My main thought about him is that he's too small."

"Too small?" she asked.

"To have been the guy I fought and Marcie took a couple of shots at. Of course, if he was wearing a complete pro football outfit, he'd gain two inches and forty pounds, but that costume would be a bit much even for a mad killer. And when I laid a right into the guy's middle, I hit muscle and ribs, not padding. There *is* a difference, one you can feel."

"I'll take your word for it."

"Jack *is* big enough, but he's never been athletically inclined. If he has muscles he's kept them a damn good secret. So," Donovan said with a loud sigh, "all things being equal, I'll get on with looking for Mr. X."

"And what about Marcie?"

"She's still the main part of the plan. I'm sorry if that upsets you, but I'm serious about this investigation. Marcie is the best. I don't want to have to say it again. Last night's little extravaganza in no way compromises her as a decoy. The shadowy figure she pegged a couple of shots at can't have seen her as being more than some kind of cop. He had to have been ducking bullets, not checking to see if the person shooting at him was a chick. If anything, he thought she was me. She *is* about my height, and *did* run into the park in one of my sweatshirts. So what if her tits are bigger?"

"You're beautiful," Rosie said, walking around her Formica kitchen table and resting her head on Donovan's shoulder.

"You don't mind having her around, then?"

"If she has the sense to like you, she can't be all bad."

"Thanks," Donovan replied, with vague enthusiasm.

Rosie took her head off his shoulder. "Why don't you go? As much as I like you, I want to get back to sleep. I had a rough night last night, and tonight doesn't look like it will be much better. The ice maker is on the fritz, the taps are about to go out, and the price of Schmidt's may go up again."

"Again?" he replied, aghast. "It's gone from sixty-five cents to ninety in two years. That's far in excess of the inflation rate, darling."

"You got your crimes," she replied, kissing him on the lips, "and I got mine."

IT WAS ABOUT TIME

All the leg work Jefferson and the expanded squad of detectives had been doing finally was turning up answers.

"It's about time," Donovan commented, sipping coffee and fiddling with the papers on his desk.

"We can't shake Jack's story, but we messed with Silver Shoes' tale a little."

"Oh?"

"He said he wasn't at the tennis courts at all on the day Camelia was murdered. Gomez says he wasn't there. However . . ."

"Gomez has his head stuck in the *Racing Form* a lot of the time," Donovan cut in.

"He's not the world's most organized person. We dug into the matter and found out he didn't spend the whole day at the tennis courts like he said the first time we asked. At three-thirty he decided to trim the weeds up on top of the big hill . . ."

"Where I found Camelia's body."

"Right. Gomez was up there from three-thirty to nearly

five, whackin' away at the poison ivy with one of those things that look like a scythe."

"There's no poison ivy on the hill, but I get your point. Who was running the tennis courts in his absence?"

"One Alfredo Battista, a CETA job trainee who was working part time."

"And didn't bother to log Silver Shoes onto a court."

"Not exactly. Silver Shoes played on the pro court. That's the one the local pro has first dibs on. Anyone can use it, but you aren't logged and the pro has the right to bounce you off if he wants to. Silver Shoes is a regular—plays nearly every day—and on the day in question used the pro court."

"Hence, he didn't have to sign up," Donovan said. "And having split by the time Gomez finished whackin' the weeds, never went down in the log as having played that day. When we asked about Johnny, Gomez used the log to refresh his memory."

"You got it, chief. I showed Battista that photo you had taken of Silver Shoes and Battista ID'd the bum right off."

"Who'd he say Silver Shoes was playing tennis with?"

Jefferson shook his head. "Battista just said it was some redheaded chick who looked quite a bit older than him."

Donovan set down his coffee cup. "The light at the end of one nasty little tunnel, my friend. Have a photo taken of Lois and show it to Battista."

"Silver Shoes and Jack's wife? You got to be kidding. No, when you think about it . . ."

"Having Lois hit the hay with our Pawnee John McEnroe explains a lot."

"One thing being why-the-fuck Silver Shoes would lie about not having played tennis that day."

"Another being why Lois was so secretive about the identity of her lover. Silver Shoes fancies himself a future U.S.

senator, right? But the problem is he's putting the wood to his college professor's wife."

"Putting the what to?" Jefferson asked.

"Wood. There's lotsa wood in Oregon. Anyway, Jack openly threatened to break his neck, and surely would have tried to get him bounced out of Columbia. That might have put an early crimp in the senatorial career."

"So both of them lie, and Silver Shoes' fellow redmen cover for them. They probably went straight from the tennis courts to bed the night Camelia Rodriguez was killed."

"No doubt," Donovan agreed.

"Then you think that Silver Shoes had nothing to do with any of the killings?"

"That's what I think."

"Okay," Jefferson said, "I'll ask both of 'em what they were doing last night during the fiery cross incident, but it will only be a formality."

A PULLMAN IT AIN'T

Riley's was thick with thieves. Rosie hit the numbers for the first time in her life, and was richer by $700. Grateful for innumerable tips on which number was lucky on which day, she began buying drinks for the house. Way before Donovan slouched into Riley's late in the evening, every deadbeat on Broadway seemed to have gotten wind of the good fortune.

"I can't believe you're doing this," Donovan said, curling his fingers around a bottle of beer.

"*Vita brevis*, baby," she said.

"You could use that money."

"I intend to, most of it, anyway. Look, William, I got

seven hundred dollars and I'm returning maybe two hundred to the community. Look at it as a kind of grant."

"The Rodriguez Foundation," he said.

"Yeah, that sounds right. Excuse me a while, would you? I got some fence mending to do in the back room."

Donovan asked what happened.

"Big Harold came in and decided to get even for the Alamo by breaking Gomez's balls. Gomez left in a huff and Doc, who was helping him pick horses, went into the back room to hide. The old guy threw up on the floor and passed out in a booth."

Donovan smiled.

"Anyway," Rosie went on, "he scared the shit out of a couple of Princeton guys who aren't accustomed to the way life works in the real world. I got to see if they're all right."

"Where's Doc?" Donovan asked.

"Still there. I threw a tarp over him."

"I'll check to see if he's okay," Donovan said. "I kind of feel responsible for the old fool. Stupid of me, I know."

Rosie offered free drinks to the Princeton men. Donovan, who suspected that they weren't so much shocked as eager to get in on the free booze, checked out the old man.

Doc was on his right side, curled up into a ball. His pure white skin was wrinkled and cold, the muscles stiff. Donovan felt for a pulse and found none.

"Oh, shit," he said softly.

JEFFERSON WAXED PHILOSOPHICAL

"They all die sooner or later, lieutenant," he said.

"He had to do it in *my* bar, when *my* girl was on duty."

"Oh, is it *your* girl again? I guess that means High Yellow is gone. You know I don't care for Spics, Bill, but I think Rosie is a better deal than your semiblack hot-shit Mama."

"I'll take that as approval," Donovan replied, watching as the morgue attendants put Doc's body onto a pallet and carried it out to the meat wagon. The death put a conclusive damper on the gaiety Rosie had tried so hard to create, and once again Riley's was nearly deserted.

"It looks like a heart attack compounded by old age and alcoholism," the medical examiner said.

"He drank himself to death," Donovan translated.

"That's about the size of it," the medical examiner said, before following the body out to the street.

Several uniformed policemen stood about, making incomprehensible scratches on small official report pads. As Rosie stayed behind the bar, tidying up and hiding, one of them came up to Donovan.

"The deceased didn't carry I.D., lieutenant," the man said, "but I understand you knew him."

"His name was Gruen, William Gruen, 170 Riverside. I don't know the apartment number."

"You don't know his age, do you?"

"Somewhere in his eighties, I imagine. And to answer your next questions, he was a retired physician and had no relatives that I'm aware of."

The officer asking the questions nodded while finishing writing. "Is there anything else you can tell me about him?"

"Nothing that matters. He was an old man who kicked the bucket. I haven't spoken to him in years. Do your own investigation, for Christ's sake. I've had enough corpses of my own lately."

That answer didn't satisfy the uniformed cops, but they

knew better than to argue with a lieutenant, especially one of Donovan's notoriety, and soon were gone. Donovan went back to the bar and reclaimed his beer.

"It's flat," Rosie said, replacing it with another.

"Nothing changes in this neighborhood. I know this guy who used to live in my building. He's an opera singer, a tenor, a big guinea with a beard and a great voice. He took a job teaching music in Stuttgart and was gone two years. He came back for a visit last summer, walked into the West End and the bartender looks at him and says 'your beer's gone flat.' I swear, Rosie, you could go to the moon, stay a decade, come back, and nobody would have noticed you were gone."

"It's too bad about Doc."

"Yeah," Donovan said. "There's lots of things I wish I could change."

YOU TWO TAKE THE CAKE

Lois and Johnny sat on Donovan's couch, nervously holding hands and looking very much like high school kids who had just been caught screwing in the broom closet.

Donovan was momentarily in a chastising mood. "I know lots of fuckups from my days drinking at Riley's, but you two take the cake," he said.

"I'm sorry, William," Lois said.

Silver Shoes said nothing, and a short silence ensued during which Donovan's mood shifted back to quiet understanding.

"Did we really mess up your investigation?" Johnny asked.

"You could say that. On the other hand, it could have

been worse. You could have *done* the murders. I'd hate to have my old friend Lois switch from a philanderer to a murderer practically overnight."

"Will it have to get out about us?" she asked.

"No. At least not if what you are now telling me is true."

"It's true," Silver Shoes said, dropping Lois's hand and lighting a cigarette.

"We were together the whole time Rosie's sister was killed. If we have to testify about it, we will, no matter what the ramifications are."

Silver Shoes nodded in agreement, though the difficulty he had lighting his smoke betrayed a wish to be in another place, another time.

"Okay," Donovan said, "let's leave it among the three of us. Nothing on paper. And nothing will ever *be* on paper as long as you two are straight with me."

Lois said that she needed a drink.

"What are your plans?" Donovan asked. "Are you going to get married, move in together, or what?"

"I don't know. Neither of us knows. Johnny is young enough to be my son."

"Not unless you got pregnant at age fifteen," Donovan said, "and that just isn't done in Oregon."

Silver Shoes laughed nervously and stubbed out his cigarette, suppressing a tobacco cough. "Will Jack have to know?" he asked. Donovan sensed he was uncomfortable saying "Jack," being accustomed to "Professor Regan."

"I don't think it will be necessary, and until it is, let's talk about something else."

"Who do you think is killing those girls?" Johnny asked.

"After a month of reasonably frantic police work," Donovan noted ruefully, "I don't have the faintest idea."

NOT HALF AS MUCH FUN

"Okay," Jack laughed, "I admit that the sexual olympics didn't turn out to be as much fun as I had imagined. I'm giving up women, did I tell you?"

"What do *they* think of it?" Donovan asked. "Did you print up ballots and take a vote?"

Lois and Johnny had left only a short while before. This time, Donovan wasn't worried about scheduling such potentially volatile encounters so closely together. He was sure the first two would be off at one or the other's place, enjoying the fruits of their newfound relief.

"There weren't *that* many," Jack said.

"And none of 'em are of voting age anyway. What were you down to, fifteen?"

"After Sonia was a girl who was eighteen," Jack said quickly. "She was a freshman at CCNY and a talented young dancer. This one wasn't a checkout girl, since that seems to bother you."

"Hey, I'm the one who's going out with a barmaid. Don't accuse me of elitism. The closest I came to college was chasing a car thief across the Columbia campus one time."

"You're smart enough. Don't pretend otherwise. Brains are important to you. If beauty was the only thing that mattered to you, you'd be married to Marcie by now."

"She has smarts. She was smart enough to leave me."

"And wise enough to come back now and then. Don't sell yourself short."

Donovan mused, "I want Marcie. I'll always want her. I know that I'll never be able to live with her, but she sure as hell can warm up a cold winter. Look, I think I'm gonna go down to the park and watch tonight's run up close. Why don't you come along? You don't have to work on your dissertation, do you?"

"Are you serious. Have you any idea what a Ph.D. in art history gets you in the way of jobs these days? . . . Sure, let's go down to the park."

But as they made ready to go, the dark figure who already had killed three girls plodded through the dripping caverns that crisscrossed under Riverside Park. He ignored the rats that scrambled across his feet and nipped at the filthy cloth strips muffling the sound of his footfalls. With single-minded passion, he made his way down into the park to kill again.

THE LAST TIME

"When was the last time you wore a bra?" Donovan asked, watching Marcie's breasts as, soaked with sweat, they shimmered under her t-shirt.

"I never wore a bra. When was the last time you wore a jock strap, Donovan? People with good stuff shouldn't be afraid to show it off."

Jack smiled, and Donovan noted it with pride. Jack was quite taken with Marcie. He was being drawn back into the world of grown-up women.

It was seven o'clock on an unusually hot May evening. Marcie had spent two hours playing basketball and drinking Colt 45 with a pickup group, all black, at the Seventy-ninth Street courts. Had the rest of the players known that the tall, muscular man with the foul mouth and the terrific hook shot was a detective sergeant in the NYPD, it would have spoiled their day. Had they known that the high-yellow chick with the impossibly good looks who had drifted into their midst like a gift from heaven was also a cop, they might never have come back.

Marcie stood in Gomez's country club at the Ninety-sixth Street tennis courts, drying off and gearing up for the evening's run. Having established herself as a park regular not only in the vicinity of the tennis courts and the basketball courts, she would now extend her nightly jogging run to Seventy-second Street where the park ended.

Jefferson was up in Donovan's apartment, using the commanding view of the park to run the show. Donovan would stay at Ninety-sixth Street with Jack, listening and waiting. Other cops were at Eighty-ninth, Seventy-ninth, and Seventy-second. Two of them, a young man and woman, both Puerto Rican, were doing a passable imitation of coitus under a blanket on the grass near the Seventy-ninth Street Boat Basin. The phony wino who had been with the stakeout since the beginning and who had also come to relish his job was now on a bench near the spot where Dubay was killed. The big black who played basketball with Marcie had acquired an immense radio and was making quite a racket in the vicinity of Seventy-second Street. Still, the coverage for Marcie was drawn out. From Eighty-ninth to Seventy-ninth, a desolate half mile, she was out of visual contact with her fellow officers. Donovan was worried.

"I'm worried," he said.

"Come on, Donovan, if you can't stand the heat, take off some clothes. You're boring me."

"I want you to wear a radio."

"I can't. Look at me, baby, it's eighty degrees out."

"Seventy."

"Whatever. The point is, it's too hot for a nylon jogging suit. I have to wear shorts and a t-shirt. And *that* is not enough to hide a radio under."

"I don't like this."

"You also don't like the Russian Tea Room and roller disco. Would you leave me some freedom for just one time? I'm a black belt. I can take *you.* "

"That's never been proved," Donovan replied testily.

"There's no time like the present," she said, pretending to square off against him.

"Come on," he said, sighing irritably and looking away.

"It's seven-fifteen," Marcie said. "I have to go. Donovan, I'll see you in a few miles. Jack . . . welcome to the ranks of the no-longer-suspected. Do me a favor and take care of this asshole for me until I get back."

"Sure," Jack said with a chuckle. After all the abuse he had taken in recent weeks, seeing Donovan humiliated was sheer joy.

Marcie left on her run. Donovan listened while Jefferson, in his damnably efficient way, had all the observation posts checked in and coordinated. Donovan felt left out. He had made the decision to keep tabs on the run from down in the park rather than from his apartment so he could be closer. Now, he seemed far away. Donovan realized that he really wanted to be near that awful iron door leading to the subterranean chamber where he sensed the presence of the man he was after. Donovan didn't know why that room fascinated him so. Surely the killer couldn't use it as a hideaway any more, what with the cops aware of it.

Marcie was past Ninety-second Street and out of sight on her way south. Donovan stuck his hands in his pants pockets and looked disconsolate.

"She's quite a woman," Jack said.

"Yeah."

"She seems very capable. You shouldn't worry."

"She's always been very capable . . . never had a self-doubt in her head, come to think of it. Maybe that's what turned me off about her. People should have things wrong with them, shouldn't they? And be able to recognize them? Well, she doesn't, and can't."

Donovan heard the radio reports as Marcie passed the checkpoint at Eighty-ninth and entered the half-mile stretch in which there was no coverage. Donovan saw that iron door opening, and his skin went as cold as the dripping passages beneath his feet. Forty or fifty feet below, a freight train rumbled on its way north from the Hudson River piers to upstate New York. The ground shook, and Donovan was reminded of the extent to which the park was a fragile green skin stretched over the frame of a beast.

He saw Marcie running to her death, with no one to help her. Donovan saw the massive, dark figure coming out of hiding, out of the very earth itself, and moving on her.

"Jefferson! Call it off!" he yelled, in a cold sweat.

The black sergeant was on the radio in a second.

"Whatsa matter, boss?"

"Tell our guys to pick her up! Now, dammit! She's alone too long!"

"Come on, lieutenant, we'll blow the whole surveillance," Jefferson protested, feebly as it turned out.

"Protect her, Goddammit!"

Jefferson hesitated, and then the radio was alive with orders. "Scrub it! Scrub it! All posts move in to protect Sergeant Barnes!"

The park erupted with shouts, orders, sirens, and imperatives, all too late. Marcie was jogging through a stand of dogwood trees halfway between the Soldiers and Sailors Monument and the Seventy-ninth Street Boat Basin when out of the dark stepped a massive figure, all black, his face rubbed with charcoal, his feet wrapped in cloth.

She looked at him, stopped, and set herself, her left hand

extended toward him, her right curled into a fist and held at her breast. *Come, sucker,* she thought, *let's get it over with.*

But the man only raised his hand, which held a .38, and silently pulled the trigger. There was a roar, Marcie was thrown to the ground, and a curtain was drawn over her.

ORPHEUS UNBOUND

Donovan knelt by her, squeezed her hands, and wept. He had sprinted three-quarters of a mile, something he hadn't done in years, and his tears were mixed with gasps for breath.

Jefferson was only a bit less out of breath. "She's alive, Bill. She's still alive. Get away and let us work on her."

The Puerto Rican cop who had feigned coitus with a policewoman near Seventy-ninth had paramedic training and was giving Marcie CPR while his partner kept the throat open. Marcie bled from a stomach wound. Blood was everywhere. As an ambulance and dozens of police cars converged on the scene, Donovan finally let Sergeant Jefferson pull him away.

"You can't help her, man. You're just in the way."

"I *want* him," Donovan stammered. "He's here, and I want him. I want every goddam door leading into every goddam underground compartment in this park covered."

"I'm doin' it, boss. Why don't you sit the fuck on the grass and let me get on with it?"

Jefferson pushed Donovan away from Marcie on to a patch of grass, and shoved him to the ground. At this point Jack ran up, even more out of breath than the rest of them.

"You!" Jefferson ordered, "you keep him here! Sit on the prick if you have to, but keep him here!"

Jack nodded dumbly, and did as he was told, pacifying Donovan while Jefferson checked on Marcie and returned with a grin. "She looks to be okay. The bullet missed a lot of vital shit. She has a long way to go before I can tell you she's as good as new, but I think she's gonna live."

Donovan said nothing. He was hunched over crying, his head between his knees.

NO TEARS FROM A STONE

Donovan hated hospitals even more than he hated funerals. In his years with the department, he had spent too many hours in hospital corridors, waiting for good news that so often turned out to be bad.

He stood alone in a busy hall, joined now and again by Jefferson, who was constantly running in and out of the chief nurse's office, coordinating the search for the man who shot Marcia Barnes.

"Heard anything yet?" Jefferson asked after one such spate of phone calls.

"No," Donovan said quietly, keeping his back to the wall like western gunfighters were said to have done.

"We found the gun. The guy tossed it into some bushes near the handball courts. It's a Smith & Wesson Chief's Special."

"Mine," Donovan said.

"What?"

"It's my gun. The one he took off me the time we fought. I can feel it."

"That's a long shot, lieutenant," Jefferson protested.

"This whole thing is aimed at me somehow. It only makes sense for him to have used my gun on Marcie."

"Unh, yeah, well, I guess we'll see about that." Jefferson took the suggestion as evidence of the stress Donovan was under, and wanted to get off the subject as fast as possible. "I can tell you one thing, though. We got men watching every goddam door in that park, with the lock team goin' around and opening 'em one at a time."

Donovan nodded.

"I mean, it's possible that dude jumped into the river and swam away. Apart from that, he's gotta still be in the park. We had cars looking for guys runnin' along the highway at the time he would have been doing it."

"Good," Donovan said.

"We also found footprints. You know, in the soft soil from that little bit of rain we had last night? They were the same as the ones the night of the Rodriguez killing. Like he had his goddam feet wrapped in rags."

"I see."

Donovan hadn't looked at Jefferson during the whole conversation. He was turning himself to stone, so he could stop crying.

"Hey Bill, maybe in a little while you and me can go out and have a few beers and try to get you settled down."

"You don't drink."

"I'll make an exception."

"Never mind. I'm sick of booze. I just want to be left alone."

"Sure thing," Jefferson said in a resigned tone. "I got to make some more calls." And then he was gone again.

Donovan kept staring at the opposite wall, where a canvas fire hose was coiled like intestines behind a glass panel. In the distance, he could hear Jefferson yelling at someone over the phone.

A doctor came up, wiping his freshly washed hands on a towel. Donovan didn't look at him either.

"She'll live, lieutenant. We had to take out most of her stomach and a piece of small intestine, but the bullet missed her spine, and that's the important thing. She'll have to learn to eat light, that's all."

"She eats light now," Donovan said, still not looking at the man.

"All the better, then."

"Can I see her?"

"No. She's in Intensive Care, and unconscious. Maybe in the morning."

Donovan turned away, then remembered something and turned back. "Give the bullet to Sergeant Jefferson when you find it."

"Here," the doctor said, and dangled a plastic bag holding a small mass of lead. Donovan took it and gave it to Jefferson.

"She's okay." Donovan said. "She'll live. It *was* my gun, wasn't it?"

"Yeah," Jefferson replied.

"Here's the bullet."

Donovan handed over the bag.

"I'm going home," he said, and walked slowly out of the hospital.

TECHNOLOGY IS NOT WITHOUT ITS USES

The new-style phones had cute little transparent four-con-
ductor cables which reminded Donovan of the wires he used
on his Lionel train as a kid. The plugs came out with the
flick of a thumb, and the telephone ceased to ring.

Donovan's doorbell was still broken. As things stood, he
wouldn't change it for the world.

AT LAST A PIGEON DEFENSE SYSTEM

After years of trying, Donovan invented a pigeon defense
system that worked. It involved a trip wire set across the
windowsill and connected to a sensitive mercury switch
cannibalized from a wall unit he found in the garbage. Despite long-standing protestations of having no talent for
electronics, Donovan could do simple things. When a pigeon tried to land on the sill, it tripped the wire that ac-
tivated a small floodlamp set outside the window. The sudden glare of the light scared the birds off. Before two days

were out, they stopped coming. After three days, Donovan missed them and took the dingus apart.

DONOVAN SPOKE TO NO ONE

Donovan stopped drinking, barely ate, and took to spending hours on the basketball courts, shooting fouls. He was, of course, fired.

Donovan wasn't actually fired. That was how he described it. Technically, he was relieved of responsibility for the case and put on sick leave. It was generally thought he had gone off the deep end.

The case was taken over by two cops from the Nineteenth Precinct which, like Marcie's apartment, was on the East Side. Donovan sat in his living room or stood on the foul line, speaking to no one. He came to wonder if he hadn't finally succeeded in proving that the world didn't need him.

ROSIE TRIED

And more than once. She cornered him at every opportunity. He was always cordial, but he wouldn't open up to her.

Jack tried, too. He entered into a conspiracy with Rosie to get Donovan to open up, to no avail. Donovan felt himself responsible for the three deaths and the near-fatal attack on Marcie Barnes. He couldn't explain it, let alone finger the man responsible. He toyed with the idea of quitting the force and taking some other job, say as a night watchman.

After a time, even Lois and Johnny were involved in the

campaign to save Bill Donovan. Every friend he had was in on it.

THE ENEMY BELOW

Donovan sat alone in the dark room, listening to the rats and the far off sound of water dripping. A votive candle bought at the local food store sat in the dirt at the center of the room where Donovan first detected the killer's hiding place. Donovan was leaning against the wall below the spot where the six-foot sewer main entered the room. The heavy iron cover was in place.

Donovan was there half a day, drinking coffee and listening. He was amazed by the number of things he could hear. There was water dripping, rats going about their lives, and every few hours, the overwhelming roar of a freight train rumbling on its way north out of Manhattan.

Of life in the park above, Donovan could hear little. When the cops drove by in the occasional squad car, he heard the event as a slight buzz. Donovan could hear when a motorcycle, a car with a broken muffler, or a siren went by on the West Side Highway. Apart from these things, he was alone with his thoughts.

"You're not alone," Jefferson said, pushing his way into the room and hurting Donovan's eyes with the bright, late afternoon light.

"Go away," Donovan replied.

"Come on, boss, this is gettin' outta hand. Here, I brought someone to see you."

Donovan looked up with wary interest as Santos Rodriguez was ushered into the room and the door shut behind him. Once again the votive candle supplied the light.

The wiry Cuban walked up cautiously, his hands in his pockets to avoid expressions of emotion which he felt might upset Donovan.

"Bill . . . I want to talk to you . . . is important."

Donovan saw that defense was hopeless. "Sure," he said.

"Rosalie . . . she need you. She alone now. She lost her sister and think she lost you. She can't take much more."

"Did he tell you to say that?" Donovan asked, indicating Jefferson.

"No. I say it on my own."

"I can't help Rosie. Camelia was murdered because Rosie was a friend of mine. Marcie was shot for the same reason. I'm the guilty party in these crimes, Santos."

"Bullshit," the Cuban said.

"What?"

"You want I say it in Spanish, Bill?"

Donovan got to his feet. "How are DiGioia and Culmone doing on the case?" he asked.

"Nothing so far," Jefferson reported.

"They should have stayed in the whorehouse. Look at this."

Donovan went to the iron cover blocking entrance to the sewer pipe. With a few grunts, he twisted it half a turn, then jumped back as it crashed to the floor.

A pint of water dripped onto the floor once the cover was off the pipe.

"So what?" Jefferson asked.

"I took that cover off two hours ago. It only weighs about a hundred pounds, despite what our astute technicians claimed. When I took it off, a few gallons of water spilled out. This time, two hours later, about a pint spills out."

"So?"

"So when we took off that cover the night of the fiery cross, no water spilled out."

"There is lot of condensation in pipes like that," Rodriguez said.

"Yeah, a pint's worth in two hours. Yet the night of the fiery cross, nothing came out. Ergo, the cover had just been on and off and any spill out cleaned up, the same way the rest of the floor was cleaned up."

"Are you saying . . .?"

"That the killer got into and out of this room . . . and, by extension, the park . . . by way of that pipe? Yeah, that's what I'm saying."

Jefferson was quiet for a time, then he said, "That *would* explain a lot."

"Damn right it would," Donovan said, a triumphant look in his eyes for the first time in a while.

"Those pipes go everywhere," Rodriguez added. "I've seen schematics for this park, and there are pipes all over the place. You could walk for miles in these tubes."

"Do you know them?" Donovan asked.

"I can figure out. You get me plans from my shop and in a couple hours I lead you through every inch."

Donovan and Jefferson exchanged glances, and the sergeant said, "You get a civilian involved and it's your ass, baby."

"He's already involved. His daughter is dead. And my ass is worthless anyway. What have I got to lose?"

Jefferson said, "All right, all right, just keep my name out of it. I got a future in this business. At least I'd like to think so. Before the two of you go off tilting at windmills, you want to clear up some routine bullshit."

"What routine bullshit?"

Jefferson opened his briefcase and withdrew some papers.

"You got to sign the on-the-scene report for the Gruen death. You were there when he cashed in, so you got to put your name on the papers."

"Gruen? Oh, 'Doc', sure, I'll sign the goddam papers."

Jefferson handed a sheaf of them to his lieutenant, and watched while Donovan looked them over. Jefferson even pushed open the iron door that separated them from the light of the outside world, and yet Donovan didn't take his eyes off the papers. After a time, Jefferson asked what the matter was.

"Unh . . . Gruen, this form says something about his name having been changed. Why does that ring a bell?"

"It's your bell, so you tell me."

"His name originally was . . . help me, I can't read your writing."

Jefferson ran a fingertip across the form to the appropriate box, and said, "Gillis. His name was William Gruen Gillis, but he dropped the Gillis after he got out of Sing Sing. He was a convicted abortionist, remember? In 1957 that kind of put a dent in your career."

"I remember it now," Donovan said. "I was only fifteen when my dad arrested him, and seventeen when he got out of prison. I never paid much attention until years later, when he started hanging around Riley's and drinking himself to death. By then everyone called him 'Doc'."

"Name changes happen a lot," Jefferson said. "How do you think your family went from O'Donovan to Donovan?"

"A lot easier than your bunch got named Jefferson," Donovan shot back.

"He's feeling better," Jefferson said to Rosie's father.

"According to the prison records you dug up, Doc has a son. I distinctly recall him telling people he had no family."

"Why is this important?" Jefferson asked, impatiently.

Jefferson shook his head and took the papers away from his boss. After looking through the material, he said, "Doc had a kid named Harold who was born in 1921, right here on the West Side. As of 1962, the date of the last parole report we have on Gruen, the two of 'em both had the same address —One-seventy Riverside, just down the block from where you live."

"Harold?" Donovan asked, "Harold Gillis?"

"What of it?"

Donovan took the papers back from Jefferson and stared at them until his eyes seemed to have bored holes straight through. He let the papers fall to the floor, then sat beside them, while Jefferson and Rodriguez watched in perplexed amazement.

"Lieutenant?"

Donovan's voice was a drone, a monotone. "The man most arrested in this neighborhood . . . drunk and disorderly, assault with intent to cause grievous bodily harm, beating up a drunk *and* his pet monkey, putting a snapping turtle in the wash water of a prominent local tavern . . . Big Harold, and his last name is . . ."

"Gillis," Jefferson said with shock and glee.

"Who also used to lord it over Doc, taking him home when he was drunk, slung over his shoulder."

"Your father made the arrest that started Doc drinking, and it recently killed him. Then what you're saying is that Harold Gillis is Doc's son and killed all those people, including Rosie's sister and the attempt on High Yellow, just to get even for what happened to Doc?"

Donovan nodded. "Harold's arrest record goes back to the forties at least. The way I see it, Doc comes out of the slammer with the intention of wiping the slate clean, even to the point of acquiring a new name. Prominent on the slate is his son, a lout, braggard, and renowned fuckup. The name goes, the son goes. Pretty soon, Doc is an alky and the son a confirmed lunatic. My God, I just remembered."

"What?"

"The girl who died after Doc performed an abortion on her—she was Cuban. I don't know why I didn't think of it before. I was fifteen, the same age as her."

"Jesus Fucking Christ!" Jefferson exclaimed.

"The man is strong enough to have done all that shit. He's a janitor—he would know all about locks and maybe even have the master key to let himself into this room. As for these tunnels, I don't ever recall seeing Gillis in the sunlight. He lives in a basement, and supposedly served aboard an American submarine during the war. Jesus, that explains the feet!"

"You mean being wrapped in rags?"

"Yeah. Submarine crews wrapped their feet in rags to muffle the sound during silent running. I must have seen it in four dozen movies and didn't think of it until just now. Jesus, Pancho, the son of a bitch is reliving his youth! He's down in those goddam caverns beneath the park thinking he's back beneath the waters of the Pacific, surrounded by darkness, dripping pipes and silent running, coming up now and then to make a score."

"That's sick shit man, really sick shit, but it sounds like you got this figured out after all. Then all the ritual, voodoo bullshit was . . ."

"Window dressing, crap he picked up along the way, having nothing to do with the true purpose. Gillis is smart enough to cast suspicion elsewhere. Gomez would carry on about the Haitians pulling the heads off pigeons in the park. And both Rosie and I talked about the case in Riley's. Gillis would sit there like a lump and no one suspected he had a thought in his head."

"And Marcie?"

"Rosie must have shot off her mouth about Marcie after that surprise meeting in my apartment. Gillis heard it. And to think I drank with the prick! I even made a pet out of the goddam turtle! I mean it, Tom, I'm on the wagon forever. The booze has caused me nothing but grief."

"Why didn't Gillis kill you when he had the chance, that night he took your gun?"

"It would have been too easy," Donovan explained. "He wanted me to drink myself to death, like his father did. And he damn near got me to do it."

Jefferson edged out into the daylight, bright even as the sun prepared to dip beneath the high-rise apartment complexes across the Hudson. Donovan and Rodriguez followed.

"Give me a couple of hours to check on Gillis and run down the schematics of Riverside Park," Jefferson said. "I'll have to make this official, you dig? DiGioia will have to hear of it, and I'll need a warrant for Gillis's apartment. I know you'd like to go charging in on your own, but you can't."

"Whatever you say."

"Lock up this place," Jefferson said, indicating the door. "I don't want some fuckin' kids coming in here."

When Jefferson was gone, Donovan and Rodriguez exchanged glances. "It's gonna take three hours minimum to do all the stuff he mentioned," Donovan said.

"I been under park before. Ten years ago, I work on railroad track. I got plans at my shop."

"Get them," Donovan said. "Get a couple of those helmets with lights on them, too. I'll meet you in an hour up on the Drive."

GONE BUT NOT FORGOTTEN

Donovan knew the doorman at 170 Riverside as someone to
nod to while walking down the drive. The building was
adjacent to Donovan's, and equally old and massive. Donovan had never spoken to the doorman as far as he could
recall, but thought he might like the man.

Peter Shaughnessy had guarded the door of 170 for ten
years. A short, fat Irishman with a red face, he wore an old
brown cardigan sweater on all but the hottest of days and
drank Paddy's from pint bottles stashed at various conve-
nient spots around the building.

Shaughnessy smiled one of his slightly drunken smiles
when Donovan walked up, extending his badge.

"I'm a police officer. I run the West Side Major Crimes
unit on Broadway above the pawn shop."

"Oh, I know you're a cop. Your doorman told me all
about you."

They shook hands, and Donovan wished he had the time
to find out what his doorman had been saying about him.

"Where's Harold?" Donovan asked.

"Gone," Shaughnessy said with a shrug.

"Gone?"

"Haven't seen him in two days. Not since Dr. Gruen died."

"When he took off, did he say where he was going?"

"He didn't say nothing. He just hasn't been around. Maybe he took off in the middle of the night, but then the night doorman would have seen him. Maybe he's still in his apartment. I knocked on the door a couple of times, but there's no answer."

"Did he ever do this before?"

"Nope. He was always around. There are a lot of leaky faucets to be fixed. But you know, he never let anyone into that apartment, not as long as I've been here."

"Not even Dr. Gruen?"

"Doc wouldn't go down there. He wouldn't go into the *basement*, even. Harold's not all there, you know?" Shaughnessy said, tapping a fingertip on his temple.

"I know."

"Especially this year. Ever since spring."

"What happened this spring?" Donovan asked.

"Beats me what could have set Harold off. The only thing unusual that happened here is Doc told everyone he had had his heart checked and the guys at the hospital told him he only had a few months to go. I guess they were right, though I don't see why that should bother Harold. Doc and him never talked."

"Okay," Donovan said, shuffling his feet. "I have to get into Harold's apartment, but I can't do it without a search warrant unless you tell me you're worried about him."

"I'm worried about him, all right," Shaughnessy said. "I'm worried he might come back."

Shaughnessy kept a pint of Paddy's tucked in between the folds of the fire hose in the lobby. He opened the door of the hose compartment, took out the bottle and had a swig.

"What if there's a fire?" Donovan asked.

"Ain't never been a fire," Shaughnessy replied, wiping his mouth on the sleeve of his cardigan, "but I use the bottle all the time. You want a little eye-opener?"

"I don't drink," Donovan said.

The doorman's smile sharpened, and Donovan realized then what his own doorman had been saying about him. He didn't care. That part of his life, at least, had changed.

THE WAR HERO

The doorman's valor ebbed as the moment neared to break into Gillis's apartment. The apartment was next to the laundry room, and smack against the west wall of the cellar. The basement was immense and dark, with narrow corridors skirting the boiler room, which was mammoth and rumbled ominously like the engines of a warship. Roaches the size of mice scurried about.

"I don't know why he has the place so locked up," Shaughnessy said. "Harold is strong as an ox. I don't know anyone who would go in there."

"The point is, no one would come out," Donovan said, a remark that went unappreciated.

He used a crowbar on the door. The only key Shaughnessy found in the key room was insufficient to undo the half-dozen locks. As the doorman stood at a respectful distance, Donovan snapped the last one.

"There we go," Donovan said, flattening himself against the wall and drawing his revolver. The crowbar clattered to the floor, making a jarring sound that carried throughout the basement.

Upon seeing the gun, Shaughnessy moved even farther away. "Hey, you . . . unh . . . didn't tell me about all this."

"No, but you're not surprised, are you?"

Shaughnessy shook his head. "Would this be for those murders in the park? I saw you on the TV where you said you was out workin' on that."

"Let's say I want to talk to Gillis about it."

Shaughnessy nodded nervously, and Donovan sensed he wanted to get back to the warm comfort of his fire hose.

There was a light on in the apartment, and Donovan nudged open the door with the muzzle of his .38.

It was silent inside. Though the apartment was large, only one bare bulb was lit, and in the living room, a good distance from the door.

Donovan dropped to a crouch and moved into the apartment, staying close to the wall of the entrance foyer until he was in the living room. The room itself spread out before him like the wings of a vampire bat. He checked the other rooms and found them unoccupied, then returned to the living room and holstered his gun.

Gillis's apartment was a shrine to a life spent stumbling in and out of madness. Every square inch of wall in the living room was covered with newspaper clippings and photographs ripped from magazines. Some of the clippings were new; others yellowed with age. Donovan stared at a tattered front page from the old *New York Mirror* which bore a photo of William Gruen Gillis shackled to a blue-suited detective and the headline ABORTION DOC CONVICTED. Not far from the old front page was a picture of Donovan's father being commended by Mayor Wagner.

More recent clippings told of the three murders and the attack on Marcia Barnes. Donovan stared breathlessly at a juxtaposition: next to the photo of his father was one of himself, taken by the *Post* at his most recent press conference.

Elsewhere in the apartment were testimonies to the only period in Gillis's life where, for a time, things seemed to go well. Plastic models of American submarines, bought at Woolworth's and clumsily made, were set in front of color photographs and drawings of battle scenes. The apartment's only bookshelf was packed with histories of World War II, including a twenty-volume set bought in installments at the supermarket. A two-foot model of the Japanese battleship *Yamato* sat atop the bookshelf. A votive candle burned beside it.

The bedroom walls were decorated with pornography, most of it showing Hispanic or light-skinned black women. Donovan turned away from the room and called Shaughnessy into the apartment. The man trudged warily through the rooms, then shook his head and looked down. "Why all the stuff about Doc?" he asked.

"Harold was Doc's son."

"Then he *is* the man who's been killing those little girls."

"It kinda looks that way," Donovan said.

"I feel sick, lieutenant. I had no idea this was going on in my building. I got to go."

"Wait a second. Did Gillis have any other rooms in this building he wouldn't let people into? Say, against the west wall?"

"The wall facing the park? Yeah, there's an equipment room he won't let anyone into. You want to see it?"

Donovan broke into that room using the same crowbar. The equipment room (a misnomer, as all the building's equipment was kept in the boiler room) was nonetheless busy with stuff. There were two drums of home heating oil, both with screw tops. One drum had been tapped recently, and the sweet smell lingered in the room. Two boxes of rags that had been torn into strips sat next to an equal amount of old t-shirts, underwear, and socks.

As he examined the contents of the room, Donovan found a bag of hulled Indian corn, three dozen votive candles, one of them recently lit, piles of old clothes, all of them dark or dyed black and, most ominously, a partially used box of Remington 12-gauge shotgun shells. A six-foot sluice cap, identical to the one Donovan had so laboriously removed from the sluice deep down in the park, was set onto a pipe which projected slightly from the west wall.

"What's this?" Donovan asked.

"Why, that? That's *old*, lieutenant. They had one just like it in the building down the drive where I used to work. That goes back thirty or forty years, to the time when Con Ed thought to provide access to the cables and gas and steam lines under the drive and the park through the basements of the bigger buildings. So's they wouldn't have to be diggin' up the street all the time, you see? Con Ed built a few, and this is one of 'em." He laughed. "It's never been used."

"Hasn't it?" Donovan said.

FORGOTTEN CULVERTS AND SLUICES

"There it is, Bill," Rodriguez said, placing a fingertip atop the small, half-inch square that indicated the existence of a hidden and forgotten room reachable through the less hidden but equally forgotten culverts and sluices running beneath Riverside Park. The room, which the map showed as having the domed ceiling of a Romanesque church, was up against the underground railway tracks and was listed as a storage and access area for the railroad's water removal system.

"That's it, huh?"

"You ask me if there's a room you can get to through these pipes. That's it."

Donovan squinted at the map, barely visible in the rapidly waning evening light. They were on the upper mall, with the schematic drawing spread across a park bench, surrounded by men. When Rodriguez had come back from the subway shop at 207th Street, he brought along the equivalent of a posse. The men, all track workers, Hispanic, and carrying the biggest wrenches they could find, hedged about Donovan waiting for the signal to advance. He would have to disappoint them.

"He's in there," Donovan said. "I can feel it. And the candle he left burning proves he's waiting for me."

"We get him, then," an anonymous voice said.

"No. *I* get him. He wants to kill me. In a way, it's my fault, or my father's fault, that Camelia is dead."

"Santos told us the story," another voice said. "Is no your fault, or your father's. We get him, all right."

Donovan shook his head. "You get him, you go to jail. I get him, I get another medal from the mayor. No, my friends, you have helped enough. You watch the exits, like I asked, and I will go in after him."

"And if he kill you?"

"He won't. I lead a charmed life. And if he does? Well, then I'm no worse off than Camelia."

"You catch him," yet another voice chimed in, "and take him alive, some lawyer get him off. He be on the streets again in a year."

Santos Rodriguez waved a tired hand, and his crowd of friends fell silent. "Bill made me a promise. I think he keep it. We do as he asks, and see later."

Donovan accepted a pregnant glance from Rodriguez.

"Block the exits like I said, and trust me to get him for you. When Jefferson shows up . . . and he will, before long . . . fade into the darkness and don't argue. I'm gonna come out of this alive, but on the odd chance I don't, tell Rosie. . . . Oh, never mind."

"I know what to tell her," Rodriguez said quickly.

"Of course you do. Stupid of me to think otherwise. So long, now." And Donovan took his helmet, flak jacket, and map, and went across the drive and into the basement of 170.

DONOVAN BETS HIS LIFE

"You're a crazy man. You're gonna be buying me drinks for the rest of my life for putting me through this."

Donovan helped Little Harold down from the sluice and out of the flak jacket and miner's helmet. "I'm not worried. You keep drinking the way you do and you're not gonna live that long."

The small man brushed himself off. "I plan to live long enough to drink you broke," he said.

"Keep your mind on business, would you?" Donovan said. "Tell me about the sluice. Am I gonna fit in there?"

"Yeah, you'll be okay. This pipe runs west under the sidewalk and down below the street. It joins up with a north-south Con Ed tube that's big enough for an army. I could have been killed, you know? Gillis could have been in there."

"No way. It's too close to the surface. He wants me deep down beneath the park . . . on his turf."

"Are you sure he's down there? He coulda slipped out of the building when nobody was looking."

"The door was locked, chained, and bolted from the inside, and there's no other way out of here. And what about the candle I found burning? It hadn't been lit more than an hour or two."

Little Harold nodded in reluctant agreement as Donovan adjusted his own miner's cap, flak jacket, and revolver. "According to the schematic of the park, there's a pipe leading from the Con Ed tube west to the uncompleted sewer culvert that angles down to the bottom of the park. He's in that room down by the end of it. I'm willing to bet my life on it."

"Baby, you *are* bettin' your life on it."

Donovan offered an all-in-the-line-of-duty shrug. "Look at it this way. If Gillis is anywhere but in those pipes he would have to be the Invisible Man, and the son of a bitch don't look like Claude Raines to me."

Donovan pulled himself into the sluice. Little Harold helped him with a hefty shove from behind. Donovan turned to face his friend, who no longer looked as angry as he seemed when dragged, kicking and screaming, from his barstool at Riley's to be a consultant on tight places.

"Go back to the bar and keep my place warm for me," Donovan said.

"Hey, you don't have to buy for my whole life. That was just a joke. It'll be fine if you pick up my tab today."

"Consider it done."

Donovan turned back into the pipe and started crawling down it. "You'll take care of yourself, won't you?" Little Harold said. "I mean, I got money tied up in you."

"Yeah, yeah," Donovan replied.

RUN SILENT, RUN DEEP

Donovan was struck by the lunacy of it all. He thought about Gillis the teenager who had joined the submarine service, one of the most maddening ways to fight a war. He had endured the dank paranoia of a submarine crewman, though not, Donovan thought, as the hero he later made himself out to be. Something, either the solemn darkness of the sub or the lurking presence of the enemy, had changed Gillis. He began getting arrested, and soon was back home in the States, to live with a dying mother and a drunken father. Then a Cuban girl and an arrest by Donovan's father sent Doc into a long slide to an alcoholic death. Somewhere along the line Gillis was hauled back to the days of his youth. There were victories then; he may not have sunk the *Yamato* as he claimed, but he had victories nonetheless.

Donovan wondered if the prick could really think himself back on a submarine. During his Police Academy days, Donovan had sat in on courses in abnormal psychology at the John Jay College of Criminal Justice where bizarre things were brought to his attention. There was the burglar who attained orgasm at the moment he broke into an apartment. And the young man who shotgunned to death his entire family, believing them to be alien life forms who had abducted his kin and taken their shape. Next to them, Gillis's delusion seemed rather on the tame side.

Now Gillis was skulking in the dripping caverns beneath the real world, rising now and then, always at night, to claim another victim from the ranks of those who brought his father to ruin. It all made a mad sort of sense to Donovan as he crawled down the pipe to the Con Ed tube. The service tube was six feet wide, nine feet high with a domed ceiling, and ran beneath the southbound lanes of Riverside Drive.

There were manholes at 88th and 91st, but the section in between was sealed off by steel doors that locked from the outside. Faint fifteen watt bulbs burned continuously as Donovan wiped the grime and water from his pants, and stretched his legs.

Down the middle of the corridor, with two-foot clearance on all sides, were huge electrical conduits, steam and water mains, all separated with the usual insulation. An inch of water covered the black cement floor. Rats splashed through the water.

Thirty yards to the north, Donovan found the access tunnel which connected the Con Ed tube to the uncompleted culvert which descended at a forty degree angle, following the slope of the park, several hundred feet down to the lower mall, where it joined a horizontal tube of similar proportions. The access tunnel was dry. On his knees and elbows, Donovan inched his way down its fifty-foot length, and as he did so the rumble of the cars on Riverside Drive gradually faded into silence.

In the sloping culvert, there were steps for the workmen. Donovan switched on his helmet lamp long enough to see it would be a long, hard descent if he did it on his feet in the dark. He switched off his helmet lamp and sat down. If he made the descent sitting down, feet first, he could do it in total darkness, and he would be less of a target.

Slowly, his gun in front of him, Donovan inched down the pitch-black culvert, feeling more naked than at any time in his life. Gillis had a shotgun with him. There had been cartridges in the basement of 170 Riverside, and a registry slip from the Firearms Control Board, but no gun. Donovan knew that one blast from that 12-gauge fired up the culvert would pretty much clear it. Even sitting, he couldn't escape all the pellets.

It was deathly quiet in the culvert. Even the rats were gone. Now and then, condensation formed into a pellet of water and fell from the roof. The only other sounds Donovan heard were those he made himself as he worked his way downward. His heels scraped the stone steps and his clothes rustled over them. His breath seemed thunderous in the culvert, where everything echoed.

Donovan counted steps, figured feet, and stopped at the halfway point. He sat still and listened. Apart from his breath and the water dripping, all was silence. He couldn't see anything in any direction, and switching on the helmet lamp was out of the question. Donovan thought of dark places. He thought of his early morning movie favorite, *The Third Man.* He recalled the night when, as a rookie, he had stalked an armed suspect in the alley behind a meat packing house on 125th under that elevated portion of the West Side Highway. He thought of how his father died, shot in the pitch-black hallway of a Harlem "shooting gallery," a tenement given over to drug use. He started moving down the culvert once again.

There were two levels beneath the lower mall. The first was that level where the tracks of the Penn Central Railroad wound their way north from the freight piers of Manhattan to the rest of America. The second lay beneath the tracks, and consisted entirely of the never-used sewer lines. A short distance up the sloping culvert from the point where it joined that horizontal grid, another four-foot access tube split off from the main pipe to join the first level. There, the Penn Central had built a storage and access room from which it could tap into the sewer system. Like everything else in the system, it had never been used for its designed purpose. That storage room was the conning tower of the underground system. From it, one could reach the surface three ways: from the tracks, and their access doors; through the basement of 170, and from the empty room by the West Side Highway where Donovan first got onto Gillis's escape routes. If the killer was anywhere beneath the park, he would be in that storage room that the Penn Central had built and never used.

When Donovan got to the split-off point, he stopped. He heard something, music played softly in the distance. There was the mournful sound of a harmonica; it cut through the empty caverns like a straight razor. Donovan wondered if the tune wasn't 'Lili Marlene.' *Gillis*, Donovan thought. He inched his way into the access tube.

CANNONS IN THE RAIN

There was finally light, a slight, flickering light.

Donovan smelled candle wax and lay still, ten feet from the end of the tube, trying not to breathe. The harmonica was loud now, slightly out of tune, and the music sounded drunken. Then it stopped, the tune over, and there was only water dripping.

Donovan held his breath. He heard a sound like a man getting to his feet, and then nothing. The pause was murderous. Donovan knew why. Gillis was a sub man, familiar with silence. In the world of his victories, the slightest sound meant death. No matter how quietly Donovan thought he was breathing, Gillis could hear him. To wait was to die. Donovan seethed in angry desperation as he charged forward, on elbows and knees like an old infantryman.

Suddenly the light from the candle was blocked. A huge figure loomed in the exit portal, wielding a shotgun.

"I got you now, Donovan," Gillis said, and fired both barrels.

Donovan screamed as the pellets tore open his shoulders, back, and legs and peppered his helmet and flak jacket with holes. He emptied his revolver down the tunnel and was answered with a bellow louder than his own.

There was silence again, broken only by the desperate metal-on-metal sound of Donovan reloading his Smith & Wesson. Several shotgun pellets had pierced the skin of his face, and blood trickled over his lips. He slammed shut the magazine of the .38, inched forward, and just then he heard a low moan and the sound of a steel door being flung open.

OFFERINGS

An inexpensive card table, ready-printed with a checker-board, sat in the center of the room. There was no other furniture, nothing at all, just a rusty old harmonica that had been tossed into a corner. There were provisions: food and drink. The air smelled of candle wax and rye whiskey.

On the card table, five votive candles were arranged at the points of a chalk star surrounding a pewter chalice half filled with dried blood. The blood was old, caked, and cracked, and looked like the pictures Donovan had seen of the surface of Mercury. The chalice itself was undistinguished, being old and unpolished. Strange, Donovan thought; he had expected better.

There were footfalls beyond the exit door. Their echoes were deep and sustained. Someone was running down the Penn Central tracks. Though bleeding from dozens of tiny wounds, Donovan gave chase.

There were four tracks in two parallel, domed tunnels. Across them, four archways, barred and grated, gave Donovan a glimpse of the outside world. He saw the lights of the high-rise apartments on the other side of the Hudson, and their reflection in the water. The tunnel was dimly lit by the amber signal lights of the Penn Central. The footfalls were receding, their echoes coming more slowly.

Gillis was a block away, running south on the outermost track. His steps were laborious, his breath heavy. He coughed with every other gulp of air as blood came up from the hole Donovan's bullet had put in his lung. Donovan ran after him.

Donovan was running easily, spacing his footfalls between railroad ties, the surface wounds from the shotgun pellets forgotten. The days off the booze and the hours spent on the basketball court were serving him well. The distance between Gillis and him closed rapidly until they were only a few paces apart.

Gillis stumbled and nearly fell. He turned, panting, blood spilling down his chin. The shotgun was a twig in his massive right hand. Barely out of breath, Donovan pulled up short.

Gillis went to speak, but the only thing that came up was more blood. It covered the front of his worn brown work shirt.

"Drop the gun," Donovan ordered.

"Donovan," the man replied, his voice an infuriated gasp. He raised the shotgun slightly.

"Don't!"

Gillis's eyes blazed and he jerked the gun upwards.

Donovan fired his .38 once. Gillis lurched backwards, hit in the stomach, and dropped the shotgun. The sound of

Donovan's shot echoed up and down the tunnel, seeming to go on for miles.

The big man faltered, two slugs in him already, but stayed on his feet, grinning evilly. Donovan remembered an article he read in *Field & Stream* where a hunter gave a curious admonition on the subject of shooting tigers. The problem with killing one, the hunter said, is that there's a gap between the time the creature's brain accepts death and the time its muscles respond. In that instant, an attacking cat can travel ten yards, all teeth and claws.

At that moment, Gillis let out a bellow of blood and rage and leaped toward Donovan.

Donovan fired again, and this time the man fell onto his face and shivered.

TENTATIVE APPROACHES

Donovan sat against the outer wall, in one of the tombstone-shaped recesses where workmen stand while a train rolls by. He sat there for something less than twenty minutes. He watched a small brown rat make tentative approaches to Gillis's body, only to be repeatedly chased off by a larger rodent.

After a time, the small rat learned the advantages of caution and let the big one investigate the corpse. Once the dominant animal was absorbed nibbling on a particular spot, the other could move in. Donovan was amazed by how quickly rats learn.

He shot them both.

JEFFERSON WAS LIVID

Donovan made his way to the Con Ed switching room where he had first discovered the underground network of culverts. He found it and the surrounding area alive with cops, reporters, bystanders, and the portable floodlights that had practically become a nightly occurrence in Riverside Park.

He was weak from loss of blood and the letdown that inevitably follows the thrill of conquest. He was also covered with blood. This looked worse than it really was, for the dozens of tiny wounds spilled just enough to make him look half dead without really endangering his life. When he emerged from the underground, the first person Donovan saw was Jefferson. The black sergeant, Donovan's oldest friend, was incredibly pissed off.

"You crazy fuckin' honky, what the hell you think you doin'?"

"Sorry I'm late. I'm always late for parties."

He forced a smile and tried to take a step out into the night, but a wave of weakness swept over him and he collapsed into Jefferson's arms. A hush went up from those standing around as Donovan was carried to a comfortable patch of grass.

"You okay, man? You look like shit."

"You have a way with words, Pancho. I feel like shit. I got a couple of shotgun pellets in me, fortunately nowhere important. He fired into one of the culverts while I was crawling down it. There were a lot of BBs flying around. He got me mostly in the arms and shoulders. I didn't get shot in the ass, which saves what's left of my dignity."

"Did you get him?"

"Yeah, the body is on the tracks somewhere near Seventy-ninth. You better get him out before the goddam rats eat him."

Jefferson gave the appropriate orders, then sat on the grass beside Donovan.

"You were right about him, Bill. He *was* Doc's kid. We found papers and all kinds of shit in his apartment confirming it."

Donovan nodded, and told Jefferson about the underground room and all the things in it. The sergeant absorbed the information, then stood and brushed himself off.

"I got to go. I've ordered an ambulance. Try to stay alive until it gets here." Jefferson offered a big, toothy grin and added, "Nice work, boss."

Donovan leaned back on his elbows. The world was swimming about him. A television news crew tried to come up close, but was pushed back by uniformed patrolmen. Santos Rodriguez appeared by Donovan's side and took one of his hands, squeezing it tightly.

"I promised you, didn't I?" Donovan said, and fainted from loss of blood.

EVEN SAVAGES GROW OLD

Donovan's arms and shoulders were bandaged and wrapped with gauze. So was a portion of his shoulder blades. Here and there, yellow salve leached through the bandages. He sat propped up on two pillows, his hospital room at St. Luke's offering a fine view of Harlem.

The television was tuned to "Rat Patrol," but the sound was off. Donovan had heard enough gunshots for ten lifetimes. He was just awake after a long, sedated nap, and he had a visitor.

Marcie Barnes still managed to look good, despite her crutches and white hospital gown. She had the crutches bunched together, and was leaning on them as if she were in a TV commercial and they were a prop.

"How the mighty have fallen," she said, shaking her head slowly from side to side.

"Whatsa matter, Yves St. Laurent doesn't have a line of hospital gowns?"

"Come on, Donovan, it's not funny. Not even a little bit. You ought to see the scar on my stomach."

"Let's see it," he said.

She started to raise her gown then thought better of it. "No. Nobody's seeing this. Not ever. It's ugly."

"That policy is going to cause some problems."

"People screwed with their clothes on in the Dark Ages," she said. "And I don't *have* to wear a bikini. Still, it's a damn shame. I had a nice body before all this."

"You still do. The scar will heal. It will probably even turn out to look sexy. And as for not having a stomach, you never ate anything heavier than Perrier and broiled trout anyway. Me, I'm a whole lot worse off. They took one hundred and two BBs out of me. I'm gonna look like a plague victim."

"So what? You're practically middle aged. Who's gonna look at your body anyway?"

"You can leave any time you want," Donovan said.

She moved closer, leaned, and touched his hip.

"You know how you are after you've killed someone," she said, leering. "It's a shame we have to waste it."

He looked away. "It's different this time. I'm not proud of myself. I'm hurt and tired. I no longer think I look like Christopher George. Maybe I *am* middle aged."

SUMMATION

Jefferson marched in, all brightness and efficiency, wearing a new pinstripe suit. He went straight to the chair on the window side of Donovan's bed, pausing just long enough to give Marcie a sharp slap on the ass.

"I didn't know Lena Horne was still touring VA hospitals."

"Fuck off," she muttered, to which he responded with a guffaw.

"We got it all, boss," he went on, opening an attaché case and taking out a pile of papers. "The Navy coughed up its records right away, but the old police files are stored in the old headquarters on Centre Street. Would you believe I had to get permission from the Historic Preservation Commission to get the goddam key?"

Donovan believed it.

"Anyway, Gillis's record goes back to all the way to 1939, when he turned eighteen and came under the jurisdiction of adult authorities. He was busted half a dozen times between 1939 and 1941, mostly for busting heads but also for concocting a scheme to rip off construction supplies from the Penn Central. They were doing some work on the Riverside Park tunnels, and Gillis was on one of the work crews. He found a way of shuffling papers so copper piping turned up in the basement of One-seventy Riverside and not on the tracks."

"I didn't think he had the brains," Donovan admitted.

"Gillis was a bright boy. He just had a problem with taking orders. Now, he got the chance to go into the service or go to jail, and promptly became the Navy's headache. He did two tours of duty as a mechanic—not a torpedoman, as he claimed—but saw no action *at all*. Gillis pulled the same shit he pulled in New York. He schemed and started fights and spent the rest of the war goin' back and forth from the stockade to a job workin' on subs in a concrete bunker by the water's edge in Pearl Harbor."

"I think I know the rest," Donovan said. "He came back after the war was over and made up the story of being a hero. He also wasn't reformed, which the Navy was supposed to do for him, and Doc decided to write him off as a bad seed."

"Bad ain't the word for it," Jefferson said. "That guy was

arrested at least once a year for something or another. Most of the time, the complainant was too scared of the son of a bitch to testify and charges were dropped."

"Yeah, and in recent years the sector cops have kind of assumed that anyone dumb enough to sit next to Gillis in a bar or, God knows, talk to him, deserves having his head broken. He nearly broke mine. Anyhow, it's all academic now."

"The blood in the chalice was from the three victims," Jefferson said, quieter now. "The chalice itself was nothing special, a medium expensive flower pot he might have picked out of somebody's garbage."

"And probably did," Donovan said with a sigh. "Gillis's whole philosophy was shit he picked up in the street. The guy was tailor made to be a janitor."

Donovan closed his eyes and stretched his arms. That hurt, and he stopped.

"I have to go," Marcie said, sticking her crutches under her arms. "I'm being released tomorrow, and want to get a good night's sleep."

Donovan reached out and touched his fingertips to hers. "We must do it again sometime," he said.

"Yeah," she replied, and was gone.

Jefferson let her go without comment. When Donovan and he were alone, he said, "She's not a bad girl after all. I'd go for her myself, if she wasn't so white."

"I'm a sick man and don't have time for this shit. Tell me about my legal problems."

"You don't have any. DiGioia and Culmone have gone back to the Nineteenth Precinct with commendations for having assisted in the solution of the park murders."

"What did *they* do?" Donovan asked.

"Nothing, but you ain't in a position to argue. You took after Gillis on your own, and the fact you turned out to be right is beside the point. Anyway, you're a hero again, Donovan. The *Post* has got your picture on page three."

"That's pretty good. I only got page five the last time."

Jefferson shoved his papers back into his attaché case and closed it. "It's terrific working for a hero," he said.

"Two more years," Donovan mused. "Two more years and I grab my pension and go. You can have my job then. You'll be a lieutenant. Maybe you'll get to be a hero too. A couple of years from now they might be picking BBs out of *your* hide."

"What the hell are you gonna do?"

"Go private. Work in a goddam A&P as a night watchman. How the hell should I know?"

"I got the BBs, you know," Jefferson said. "All one hundred and two of them. Every single one they took out of you. I'm gonna have them fuckin' mounted and hung on the wall behind my desk."

The shotgun pellets the doctors took out of Donovan were arranged in the middle of a plexiglass frame, in a pattern that resembled a shotgun burst. Jefferson was nothing if not a man of his word.

NORMALCY RETURNS TO THE WEST SIDE

Riverside Park was once again open to the public at all hours of the day and night. New Yorkers, quick to forget disaster, resumed using the facilities as if nothing had happened. Things became so routine that within two weeks there were four drunk-and-disorderly arrests, a flasher, a fight between a dog owner and a jogger disgruntled after stepping in shit, and a nonfatal heart attack.

Donovan got another medal. "I have more than Marshal Tito now," he observed.

"Tito is dead," Rosie pointed out.

The police commissioner forgot about Donovan's unauthorized conclusion of the case. The case was, after all, concluded. The commissioner even instructed his pretty young press aide to make up a convincing story about how Donovan's dramatic intervention was the department's idea. She wrote a masterpiece in which Donovan was allowed by his superiors to personally hunt down the mad killer who shot Sergeant Barnes and murdered three girls. It was, of course, a crock of shit, and read that way to veteran reporters. They reported it as written anyway. Marshal Tito was dead, and everyone loves a tale of heroism.

AND AS FOR RILEY'S

Nothing much changed. Three regular customers were gone, if you counted Donovan's sobriety as a lost customer. The blow was softened by the knowledge that Gillis was a pain in the ass under the best of circumstances and Doc was a bad tipper.

It was nearly closing time. Donovan sat by the end of the bar nearest the window, drinking club soda and watching the pedestrian traffic on Broadway. It amazed him how Broadway never stopped. Even at almost four in the morning, there were couples at the fruit stands, couples coming out of the subway; couples carrying six packs, hero sandwiches, and copies of the city edition of the *Times;* couples ignoring the drunks passed out on the sidewalk in front of the welfare hotel.

SO LONG, MATA HARI

The pinball company decided, for some unstated reason, to take the "Mata Hari" machine out of Riley's and replace it with a "Sharpshooter." The former pinball machine, very popular with the younger customers, featured an illuminated graphic of a busty woman who was presumably involved in some form of evil. Women shown on pinball machines are always busty. The "Sharpshooter" machine also had busty women, but it featured a western gunfighter and electronic simulation of the sounds of gunfire, horses' hooves, and so on. "Sharpshooter" was a letdown after years of "Mata Hari," and some of the student customers complained to Donovan, knowing he was a hero cop and also the boyfriend of the night bartender.

"Can't you do something about this?" one asked.

Donovan tossed his hands up. "I'm out of the hero business," he said. "You want to take on the world, you do it yourself."

SQUEEZE SOMETHING THAT DOESN'T HURT

Rosie grasped Donovan's arm and squeezed it in a loving sort of way. He objected.

"Squeeze something that doesn't hurt," he snapped. "I have a suggestion if nothing comes to mind."

"Something comes to mind," she said, holding his hand instead.

They sat atop the big hill by the Soldiers and Sailors Monument, near where Camelia had been killed. They watched the moon set under the horizon. It bisected a high-rise, sank beneath the Jersey Palisades, and still managed to look appealing.

They held hands, and she leaned her head on his shoulder. It was midsummer, and on that day, approaching dawn.

"I think I love you," she said.

Donovan didn't exactly respond. "I'm definitely going to grab my pension and retire in two years," he said.

"Why? You're good at what you do. You could make captain."

"Never. I don't know politics. You have to be good at politics to make captain. Jefferson will do it. He'll be the first black police commissioner in this city. Me, no way. If I stick around, I'll just get my head blown off like my father did. This last business was as close as I want to come. I'll retire with a good pension and go into something safe, like being a P.I."

"What's a P.I.?"

"Private investigator. Don't you watch television?"

"On television, a P.I. is always getting the shit kicked out of him."

"Fiction, just fiction, I'll guard supermarkets and track down missing husbands, and still have my pension. No one will try to kill me. No one will kill innocent people because of something my father did."

"Bill, enough of that. I don't want to talk about it any more."

Donovan stood and pulled her to her feet. He kissed her, pressing his tongue between her lips, flicking it across the points of her teeth, until they both were gasping for breath.

"Let's go home," he said.

"I want to have babies. I want your child."

"Let's *go home*. Aren't things complicated enough without marriage?"

"Who said anything about marriage? I want to have your child."

He held her. "Come on," he said, "what about your father? What would he say?"

"My father thinks you're God."

Donovan sighed, stepped away from her, thought a moment, then took her by the hand and led her out of the park.

"Weighty responsibility, that, being God. Can I sleep on it?"

Rosie nodded, smiled, thought to make a ribald comment, then changed her mind and let Donovan drag her off to his apartment.